The Chronicles of Moxie

Z. B. Heller

THE CHRONICLES OF MOXIE

Edited by: Ella Medler
        http://ellamedler.wordpress.com/custom-writers-services/
Cover Art: Cheeky Covers www.cheekycovers.com
Formatting: Polgarus Studio www.polgarusstudio.com

To my Moo.
Thank you for helping me
bring out my Moxie.

mox·ie

'mäkse/

noun informal

noun: moxie

1. force of character, determination, or nerve

"She wore that fugly dress? Boy, she's got a lot of moxie!"

Prologue

My name is Moxie Summers. I'm sure one wonders why the hell a parent names their child Moxie. The story goes something like this. When my mother was pregnant with me, she constantly had morning sickness up until she gave birth to me. I also gave her gestational diabetes, major heartburn, kicked her ribs and sat on her bladder so she constantly had to pee. Therefore earning the name for the spawn that she bore.

I'm 5'7", have long red hair and gray blue eyes. They say that the eyes are the windows into your soul. If that's the case, people had better be able to handle the head case that they see within my soul. I am beautiful, sexy, and a size sixteen. I've never been self-conscious about my curves in the past. They just give a man a little extra flesh to grab onto when we are in the throes of passion.

With that explanation out of the way, my name is Moxie and I am being punished.

Thump, thump, thump.

Apparently, the man above me thought that me squeezing my eyes shut meant an orgasm was near. It really meant that I hoped my brain wasn't being thrown around too much and cause me a concussion.

There I was, laying there, in a bed with a mattress that was approximately 40 years old. The bed springs squeaked so loud, the noise could easily have been mistaken for barking dogs, well…more like injured barking dogs. The sheets felt like they had not been washed in about two months and I believe I just saw a spider crawl across the pillow. Wait, was that a half-eaten sandwich underneath me?

"Oh, Moxie baby, are you ready to come?"

"Umm…"

What I really wanted to say was when earth freezes over, your dick grows about 3 inches and gains about an inch in girth. I believe the name pencil dick was coined for this man. Joel lay on top of me, pushing my body into the squeaking mattress. The hair on his legs and chest was coated in sweat, ruining my beautiful triple D lilac Wahcoal bra. I was going to have to run my next wash on high heat, with extra detergent.

It was time for a choice to be made. Unfortunately, it involved faking an orgasm. Here are my thoughts about faking an orgasm. It takes way too much energy. This is energy that should be used for an all-out fuck fest. The kind of fucking that leaves you almost breathless and in pain. In order to perform a perfect faker, you have to practice your "oooo's and ahhh's" to gain a certain pitch. Luckily for me, I took improv classes, so faking was my specialty.

"Oh, baby. Yeah, do it harder," I moaned in my best fake-moan voice.

In my head: *No, seriously, do it harder.*

"Oh, I think I'm coming," I cried out in my best seventies porno voice.

Again, in my head: *Did I remember to rotate my laundry?*

"Yes! Yes! Yes!" I screamed as he did this ridiculous pumping motion into my body.

Finally, in my head: *Oh, I have leftovers from that amazing dinner Renee and I went to last night. Score!*

I believe I pulled off an Oscar-worthy performance. I just hoped Joel didn't realize I faked it, but I had two thoughts about that. One, I didn't think he ever felt a woman really orgasm, and two, his penis wasn't large enough to feel an earthquake. Then I heard something that kind of sounded like a dying cow. I was ready to go find the barn it'd come from and provide CPR, but realized it was Joel finishing his triumphant release.

Joel was what I would describe as mediocre. He would be the equivalent of going to Wisconsin Dells, when really you wanted to go to Disney World. I met him through my stepmother, who thinks she is the wisest and smartest Jewish matchmaker in Chicago. We refer to these as "Yentas", otherwise known as psychotic women with nothing better to do.

When I met Joel, he took me out to dinner at Chili's. What date can you possibly take seriously when they take you to Chili's? Maybe if I were still in high school, I would have thought it was the Ritz Carlton, but as a twenty-six-year-old adult, it was a disappointment. To add insult to injury, he suggested we split the check. Our conversation during dinner was a little mundane and went something like this:

> Me: So, you're in finance. That must be exciting.
> Joel that Blows (my nickname for him for the purpose of this dialogue): I guess so. I didn't know what I wanted to major in college, so I picked something.
> Me: Well, do you have a passion for anything?
> Joel that Blows: My main interest in college was smoking a shitload of pot.
> Me: Then maybe you should have gone into botany or horticulture.

Since it was early spring and the weather was warming up, we walked to his apartment building, which was in Bucktown. When we got there, I had every intention of heading back to my place, until Joel asked if I would like to see his Bar-Mitzvah pictures. I knew what this really meant. It was code for I want to have sex with you, but I'm using my sad excuse of a childhood milestone to lure you in. The last thing I wanted burned into my brain was a picture of a thirteen-year-old with braces and acne. However, being that I hadn't had sex in a while, I figured this was a chance to feed the angry beaver.

We entered his apartment, which looked like someone vomited up a dorm room. There were clothes on the floor, a laptop on a desk, with what looked like a half-eaten burger next to it. His couch seemed to be a hand-me-down from his grandma or a steal from a dead neighbor. The carpet had cigarette burns in it, which I figured were from previous tenants, since Joel didn't smell like smoke. Unless the heavy drenching of cologne was masking it.

Ok, I realized that I hadn't stumbled upon gold here, not even bronze. But I was horny and my beast was getting restless. So I did what any ladylike woman would do. I closed my eyes, took a deep breath, prayed to the sex Gods, and jumped towards him, knocking him down onto his moth-infested couch. This is what led me to where I am now.

After sex, I always like to do a post-sex recap like ESPN Sports Center, with my pussy as the lead quarterback. As I lay in Joel's slimy sheets, I thought about what my newscasters would say.

"In tonight's game we had a horrific tragedy that just might put our lead player out of commission."
"Yes John, I agree. Did you see the size of the balls he was playing with? I know squirrels with bigger nuts then those!"
"I can't believe he tried to perform the backdoor play. What was he thinking?"
"John, I don't think you can score a touchdown with a cocktail-sized frank."

Joel's sprawling stretch brought me back from my play-by-play. I had to question whether he wore any form of deodorant. The odor coming from his pits smelled like a

McDonald's Egg McMuffin. I could now cross those out from my breakfast options.

"Oh, baby, that was so good." He sighed as he rolled onto his back and ran his hand over his balding hair.

Exactly what planet was he on? It certainly couldn't be earth, or in this bed. I simmered, staring at the ceiling, wondering which one of my fantasies I would be using later with my handy-dandy vibrator, Carl. Yes, I named my vibrator Carl. I needed a name to scream out during an orgasm, and Carl seemed sophisticated. That was when I thought about something that could be a solution. Well, for me anyway.

"Maybe we can bring in some sex toys, like a large, thick dildo," I said softly. But I didn't get so lucky. He heard me.

"Gross! Don't say dildo," he said with a disgusted look on his face.

Did I mention that Joel was not a fan of dirty talk or anything that seemed dirty in his mind? I tried to spice things up during our coupling, mainly because I was bored out of my mind. I threw out phrases like 'ride me hard' or 'blow your load', only to be shushed by the dirty-talk police.

Joel turned his head to me. "I'm all the pleasure you need. Why the hell would you want to do that?"

Retreat, retreat! Mayday, Mayday! What I was really thinking about was the Subway jingle, 5 dollar footlong. At this point I'd pay 1000 bucks for a foot-long.

"Well, I'm not into that kinda stuff. What's the purpose of getting something that will do exactly what I do to you now? That idea is so lame," he snarled.

Stay silent, stay silent. Don't let the crazy out of my head and into my mouth. At this point, it would come out to be verbal diarrhea, and I would just have to clean up the mess along with all the tact I had left. I stretched. "I'm super-tired now. You know, long day at work and then meeting up with you…"

I'm going to hell for all my lies. I just pray the devil has a bigger dick than this guy.

"Ok, well, I'll just put on my underwear and we can go to sleep," he said.

Underwear? Who says underwear, unless it's your old Aunt Phyllis?

"You know, I have a huge day tomorrow, with a field trip and shuffling around twenty kindergarteners. I should really get a good night's rest and I know that you'll want round two and three tonight."

Who's coming with me to hell?

"Yeah, that's fine. I'll call you tomorrow and see if we can do round two and three tomorrow night," he said.

Can a person sprout a larger penis overnight? I thought that was only Pinocchio's secret power. "Right. I think this whole week is going to be tied up. I have to go visit my grandma in hospital."

Does hell have cookies? I really hope so, since I will be there for a long, long time.

"I didn't know your grandma was in hospital. Anything I can do to help?"

If you want to go to the cemetery, unearth her body and put her in a hospital bed to cover up my lying, then sure.

"Oh, that's really sweet, but totally unnecessary. She's very frail. Skin and bones, you know," I responded, thinking of my poor grandma laying in peace in the ground.

"Well, give me a call when things settle down so we can go out again and work it like rabbits."

Oh my God, he officially scared me. Did they make disinfectant for cleaning my ears after they heard something completely disgusting?

"Umm, sure," I croaked as I got up and picked up my clothes from the floor. With that, I got dressed and walked out of his place, taking my little cotton tail with me.

Chapter One

I walked into Montgomery Elementary with coffee in one hand and a donut in the other. My work bag was falling off my shoulder due to the amount of work I was supposed to get done in the time I wasted with Tiny Tim.

Montgomery Elementary was a kindergarten through fifth grade school. It was an older school, but it had charm – if you didn't mind the asbestos seeping from the walls. It was my first job after college and at the time I couldn't be picky. I had a choice: either get a job quickly, or be an endangered slave to my stepmother and her boutique. I'd rather shovel horse shit for the rest of my life.

My best friend and fellow teacher Renee spotted me slipping into my classroom and followed me in. Renee was tall, had auburn hair, and was thin, the type of girl you would see getting nominated to be prom queen in high school. I, however, was the type of girl who would have been pulling a Carrie-like prank on her, pouring the pig blood over her head from behind stage. Yes, that's right, I'm classy.

I met Renee on my first day of teaching here five years ago. She had come into my classroom to borrow tape for her Garfield "Hang in there" poster. If I remember correctly, our conversation went something like this:

"Hi, I'm Renee. I teach fifth grade down the hall. Can I borrow some of your tape?"

"Sure. I'm Moxie. Obviously the new kindergarten teacher."

"Is that a chocolate chip muffin on your desk, next to the People Magazine?" Renee asked.

"Yup. I was reading about Heidi Klum and how she lost her baby weight in two weeks by eating nothing but kale. So I decided to start my own diet of chocolate chip muffins and see if I could put on the baby weight she lost."

"That's one way to rebel at society."

"That, and I plan on killing her in the middle of the night."

"Do you want me to bring the rope and duct tape?"

From that point on we became inseparable. She was the Bonnie to my Clyde, the apple to my sauce and the chocolate to…well, everything.

Renee stood in the doorway, eyeing my donut, knowing the true meaning behind the tasty morsel. "There is a donut in your hand, which means something bad happened. Which also means you have 30 seconds to tell me what it was before the bell rings," she said.

"If you ever tell my evil stepmother I'm eating a donut I will officially disown you. She already gives me enough shit about my diet habits and my size."

My stepmother Martha and I had a complicated relationship. Most of it was due to my weight. She had always been stick-thin, and the fact that I was not dampened the prospects of suitors in my life. This would also spoil the chances of a house full of grandchildren to taunt like she did me growing up.

Yes, I was a little thick through the hips, but I decided to love my curves instead of obsessing about them. I believed in being a strong confident woman who enjoys her chocolate donuts. If there were any skinny bitches out there that had a problem with it, I would squish them between my DDD knockers. So I kept telling myself.

"I won't tell her. She would only lecture me that I need to come over and eat since I'm too skinny. Something about it being the job of a Jewish mother to make sure everyone gets fed enough, even a Shiska."

"Yes, she has to make sure the whole world is fed. She has, however, threatened to wire my mouth shut," I explained.

"Isn't that abuse?" Renee asked.

"Not if my looks get in the way of catching Mr. Right and having many grandkids." I shrugged, suggesting that I really didn't care.

"So what happened to you last night?"

I couldn't help but squirm at the question. I was recalling Joel's bad breath when he attempted to whisper sweet nothings into my ear. Something about having sunshine stream through my hair.

"Really, there isn't much to tell. Martha set me up last night with one of her Mah Jong friends' son."

Renee rolled her eyes. "Why do you insist on going on these dates that Martha sets up? We have been through this before and we have decided that plucking out your pubes one by one would be a better choice."

Renee was right, and in this case I would have plucked out an entire bush full of hair. "Well, I ended up sleeping with him anyway. I haven't gotten laid in a long time and ivy was starting to grow on the Golden Wall."

This was true. I hadn't seen any action for a while and I was wondering if my parts were in working order. Yes, I had my collection of vibrators at home, but it's always nice to feel another human being give you an orgasm instead of something with batteries. That and the fact that batteries are becoming way too expensive.

The bell rang and the kids started straggling in one by one. Renee slipped past the kids, but pointed to me on her way out. "We are so not finished with this conversation," she said, and walked to her class.

I have been teaching kindergarten since I started working at the school. They say it takes a special person to work with kindergarteners. I, however, think I'm mentally ill. Although, it does warm my heart to see my kids grow up into young adolescents and know that my teaching didn't send them into therapy for the rest of their lives.

"Ok everyone," I waved my hands in the air like I was trying to land a 747. "Put your stuff in your cubbies, then come have a seat on the carpet for morning meeting."

Twenty little bodies scurried around the cubbies like a pack of dogs that lost their tails. I called that area "the cock fight pit" because every day the kids would try to get their favorite hook. They would peck at each other until the final cock won, which was usually Drake Finley. Let's just say this is a kid you wouldn't want to be alone with in a deserted alley. I truly believed that he was a seventh grader disguised as a kindergartner.

Finally, we were all in place and I could start teaching about some very important life lessons. Such as, be kind to each other, take responsibility for your things, and get Miss Summers her Snickers bar that's sitting on her desk.

"I hope everyone had a great weekend," I said in an animated voice. "Why don't we share what we did this weekend to start our morning meeting? Andrew, why don't you start us off?"

Andrew is a little ginger-haired boy with freckles that blur together to look like he just got back from Mexico with a nice tan. "I went to the zoo with my mom and my brother. But my brother peed in his pants, so we couldn't stay that long," he said with a hint of a lisp.

"Well, I hope you got to see some interesting things while you were there," I replied, remembering that Andrew's brother was ten.

A little girl named Riley shot her arm in the air and waved it around like she was having some kind of epileptic seizure.

I pointed at the flaying child. "Riley, what did you do?"

"My mom took me to Vagina," she squeaked. "She likes to go down there a lot."

I tried not to seem outraged. "Do you mean Virginia?"

"I said Vagina; it's one of the fifty states. Geez, Miss Summers, you should know that, you're our teacher!"

"Yes, I suppose I should," I exhaled, while rolling my eyes.

"Miss Summers?" asked a little blonde girl, Katie. Katie is my kindergarten nemesis.

"Yes, Katie?"

"You know, those shoes you are wearing are made from leather. Leather comes from cute little cows. Did you know that you're wearing dead cow?"

The whole room erupted in a chorus of "Ewwww."

"Katie, it's all about the circle of life," I said.

"You mean like the Lion King?" She looked at me with excitement.

"Yes. Do you remember what happened to Simba when he became too inquisitive with his uncle Scar?"

"Scar had the wildebeest trample over his dad, Mufasa," she responded.

"Do you know what my favorite animal is, Katie?"

"A cute lion cub?" she asked.

"No, a wildebeest." Katie's eyes grew and she had nothing more to add to the conversation.

"All right, everyone, good morning meeting. Let's go over why sticking your fingers in your nose can cause your friends to become sick one more time."

The rest of the day flew by relatively fast. I suppose that is what happens when you have twenty kids, all with attention deficit, to teach. We were able to do a lesson on the letter P, until Riley came up with the example of pussy for a word that starts with P. That was when I surrendered and offered free choice for the rest of the day.

I was eager to go out with Renee for a drink and confess about my night out with Slim Jim. I started cleaning up the room and was putting papers in my bag when the principal, Mrs. James, came into my classroom.

"Hey, Mrs. James." I held my hands in the air. "Whatever it is and anyone who said I did it, I plead the fifth."

I was lucky to work with an amazing principal. Mrs. James was a fifty-year-old mother of three teenage boys. The words boobs, babes and butts were featured in her daily conversations at home. She was also extremely smart and loved the school like a fourth child. She often had the best gossip.

"Moxie, as much as I would love to tell you that I have gossip on the music teacher, sadly, that isn't the case."

I had a quick mental image of Mr. Carmichael trying to stick his penis into the hole of a guitar. Gross.

"We have a new student starting on Monday and he will be coming to your class," she finally said.

Great, another rug rat with snot dripping out of his nose, sticking his hands down his pants to "pet his alligator".

"Lovely," I replied. "Does this child have any special needs? Any peanut, latex, pencil shaving or carpet mite allergies?"

"Don't be a smart ass. He's coming from a tough situation. His mom died last year and they are moving here from Maine," she said with a sullen expression.

"There are actually people who live in Maine? Huh, I thought that was an old wives' tale."

"Do you really have carpet mites?" She glared.

"Touché, Mrs. James."

"His name is Dillion and he'll be here Monday," she concluded as she left.

I finally grabbed my stuff and headed to Renee's room. Poor Renee teaches 5th grade and always has some story to share after a long week. Last week's story was about her catching a group of girls in the bathroom feeling each other up to see if their breasts were developing. I would never have been one of those girls, considering my boobs were fully developed at the age of five.

"Ready to go? I'm dying to get a drink at Dickies," I said as I walked into her classroom.

Renee looked a little green in the face, sitting at her desk.

"What's wrong?" I asked.

"It happened again," she sighed as she stared at the front of the class.

"No!"

"Yup! Paul stood in front of the class, giving his report with a huge boner sticking out," she said as she turned her head to glance at me, looking for support.

"Shit." I sighed. "How does he not recognize that it is socially unacceptable to stand in front of a group with a raging boner? Well, unless you're at a strip club and you're trying to get a Ben Franklin into some guy's g-string."

"I don't know, but I'm going to have to have a chat with his parents soon because the other kids won't stop snickering and are calling him Penis Pauly," she quipped.

I tried not to laugh at this, but it came out. Renee laughed with me, even though I knew she was dreading speaking to this poor boy's parents.

"That will be a rough conversation. What do you even say to a parent? Excuse me, can you strap your kid's penis down with duct tape in the morning before sending him to school?" I said sarcastically.

Renee laughed. "Or maybe I can ask them to tuck it back like drag queens do."

"Well, at least you didn't have to tell a kid to stop picking his nose thirty times today." I smiled.

"Who says I didn't?"

I gave Renee a disgusted look. "Well, come on and get your crap. There is a drink waiting with my name on it."

Dickies was a tiny bar in Chicago that no one would really ever go to unless they were already drunk on a pub crawl. The atmosphere was casual. There was a U-shaped bar in the middle of the room, bar stools surrounding it and booths encompassing the outer walls. One thing that I really liked about Dickies was Simon, the bartender. He didn't storm you with questions, but always had an open ear to listen to your shit.

It was a perfect place to chill out, and they made an amazing martini. I was really in need of one to nurse my fragile state of mind and to apologize to my Tiny Dancer in between my legs. Renee and I got into the bar and sat in our favorite booth. Simon nodded in our direction and didn't even need to ask what we were having. He was a good bar husband that way.

"So, are you going to tell me what happened with Jim or what?" Renee asked with a smirk.

"His name was Joel, but I think the name Tiny Tot suits him better." I snickered.

"Ouch! That bad, huh?"

"Let's just say that I might have had better luck with a chicken's dick."

Renee's brows raised. "Chickens have dicks?"

"Seriously?" I quipped. "You're a fifth grade teacher and you are asking me if chickens have dicks?"

"I just assumed that female chickens create an egg and lay it when they're ready," Renee replied.

"And I thought I was leading little children down the road of destruction," I said, shaking my head in disappointment.

"Moxie, I don't think your luck with men could get any worse. Do you remember Blow Job Rob?"

I looked at her with squinted eyes. "We swore we'd never speak of that again."

"Yeah, the guy who wanted you to give him head and there was this big scab on it. He claimed it was just there because he was picking at it and swore it wasn't an STD."

I groaned, recalling the story in my head. The guy was smoking hot and we were having a heavy petting session in my college dorm room. I was trying hard not to vomit from the incense trying to cover the smell of pot in the room. I was anxious to see the package that this guy was carrying because I'd heard major rumors from different girls on campus. That should have been my first clue that he had been around the block a few too many times.

We got to the part where I met his Johnson and I could tell something was off right away. His size was definitely impressive, but there was a large oozing scab on his shaft. He tried pushing my head down for me to blow him and between the smell of the room and his monster wound, I ended up puking all over his lap. Needless to say, there was no second date.

"Or what about Hand Job Bob who came all over your hands before you even touched him?"

"You know pre-ejaculation is a real and serious problem in today's men." I laughed as Simon set down our drinks.

"Whatever the fuck you two are talking about just made my penis crawl into itself," he said as we both took sips of our drinks.

Renee and I clinked our glasses in a cheers and I began to drown my worries away.

A few hours and way too many drinks later, I was slightly tipsy. Ok, that was a lie. I was piss-ass drunk. Renee didn't drink that much, as she'd offered to be tonight's designated driver. That, and she knew I was desperately trying to erase the memories of ghosts of penises past.

"And what made that guy think that waxing his balls was sexy? Does he like pain? Does he think that smooth balls makes it easier to suck on?" I yelled in my drunken stupor.

Did I mention that I'm a loud stupid drunk?

Renee laughed. "I think you should take a bar poll about hairy balls."

"Exactly!" I slammed my hand on the table. "These are very important issues that must be discussed. Fuck foreign policy, if they have hairy balls, then they shouldn't be running countries!"

Right then the bar door opened and a very fine looking specimen walked towards the bar. He was all man from the top of his head to the bottom of what had to be a size sixteen shoe. He was tall, about 6'4", with brown hair, cut short on the sides and messy on top. His hair screamed *I really don't give a fuck, but I still look perfect anyways.* He was wearing a blue button-down shirt with its sleeves rolled to his elbows and that showed off his thick biceps, and jeans that curved perfectly around his firm ass. He also sported a five o'clock shadow on his face that I wanted to lick all over.

I pointed a finger at him.

"Hey, you!" I yelled. "Yeah, you with the tight ass. Do you have hairy balls or smooth balls?" I staggered out of the booth towards him.

"Excuse me?" the Adonis said. His ocean blue eyes were gazing back at me and had me breathless. Well, I think it was one pair of eyes. Again, the alcohol was having an impact on me deciphering between human and alien.

"Smooth or hairy? Lay it out for me," I slurred. The room looked like it was starting to sway a bit.

"Umm, last time I checked I didn't think it was appropriate to talk about someone's balls." He smiled, playing along.

Dear God. When the Adonis smiled, it was like the gates of heaven opened and the heaven lights shone down upon him. A choir of angels was singing and little cute cherubs flew around shooting arrows. Or maybe that was a fly buzzing by. Again, I wasn't quite sure because I was so wasted.

"Testicles are an important part of the human body," I continued to ramble. "They hold the special sauce that makes babies, and babies are cute."

"I'm pretty sure I'm familiar with the workings of the male testicles, considering I'm a man."

"I know you're a man!" I screeched. "But all men suck and they don't like the word dildo!"

The Adonis moved so close to me that I'm sure he was able to smell the multiple martinis I had consumed. He smelled divine, like musk and sweet cologne. He spoke softly, so only I could hear him. "Well, maybe those men don't know what kind of pleasure you can give a woman using a dildo, while she begs you for the real thing."

Holy shit. I stared at him, speechless. My whole body started to burn and I felt my cheeks flush. I didn't quite know how to respond to that, so I said the first thing that came to my lips. "I like pussies."

"Excuse me?" He smirked, putting one hand in his pocket and the other on the bar.

"I mean puppies! Puppies are cute and you're cute. You remind me of a dog, a big wet slobbery dog. Maybe one of those bulldogs with the spiked collar."

At that point my foot was so far implanted into my mouth, I could taste my toenail polish. After that, there was no backtracking. I could only go out with my head held high and my tits pointing out.

"Well, sir, thank you for taking part in the poll of the week at this lovely establishment. Simon, this nice man deserves a drink." I quickly walked back to the booth where Renee was trying, not very hard, to hold back her laughter.

"How bad?" I asked.

"Well, on a scale of one being an embarrassment to ten you being a complete stupid fucker, I would give it a fifteen."

"Why didn't you shut me up, you wench?"

"And miss out on the very important bar poll? Never." She laughed.

I dared myself to look back at the Adonis, who was now sitting at the bar, shooting the shit with Simon. Even though I was drunk enough not to feel my feet, looking at this man made my cocoon of love stir and I wanted his caterpillar nestled in it.

Renee pulled me out of my butterfly-themed daydream. "So, Moxie, are you going to give Joel another shot?"

"Another shot of what? Steroids to make his dick grow larger?" I sneered.

"I thought steroids are supposed to make your balls shrink," Renee said thoughtfully.

"In that case maybe he needs some of that mutant shit that Superman takes."

"You mean kryptonite? I thought that stuff kills him."

"My point exactly," I mumbled.

"Listen, why don't I drive you home and we can put on a sappy romantic comedy and eat all those Girl Scout Thin Mints you have?" Renee smiled.

I did have a large number of Thin Mints. My student, Katie, was selling them at school. I told her I couldn't buy any, that I was watching what I was eating. She then said she was also watching what I was eating and the Snickers I had at lunch looked pretty good. Since when was it ok to blackmail your teacher? She made a killer sale on that one.

"I have a better idea. Why don't we go to my place, watch porn and make fun of fake boobs and fugly men on there? Oh, and also eat all the Thin Mints I have."

"Sounds like a plan," she laughed.

We both got up from the booth and started to head out. As we were walking out, I caught the Adonis's eyes burn into me like a branding iron. I started to feel the world spin, thinking that his beauty was making the earth's axis turn.

"Thanks again for taking part in my very informative poll," I said to him, slugging his shoulder.

"And what do I get for adding my two cents?" he said, taking a long sip of his beer.

Oh, so he wanted to play hardball? Well, I had hope something of his was hard. I watched his lips as they curled around the glass. His lips were smooth and all I wanted to be was the chapstick he used to make them that way. In my mind, I imagined those lips tasting and drinking in the wetness between my legs.

"You get the knowledge that you've made a difference in the world of hairy balls," I slurred, wanting to lick the beer from his tongue.

He stood up from the bar stool he was sitting on and stood in front of me. His massive frame didn't scare me. In fact, it made me want to climb all over him as if he was a jungle gym. "What's your name?" he asked, brushing a piece of hair that was stuck to my cheek.

The room started to spin very quickly when he touched my face. I was about to answer him, but instead of words, I threw up all the drinks that were meant to erase the nightmares of my dating life. Right in front of my Adonis's feet.

Chapter Two

Monday morning came quickly after I spent the weekend hiding from the world. I could not believe what'd happened at Dickies the other night. Even though I'd been piss-ass drunk, I still remembered some of it. The memory of the Adonis had my insides turning. Both at the thought of how gorgeous he was, and the fact that I vomited all over him. All I could remember after that was Renee getting me into the apartment.

"Good morning, sunshine," Renee called as I was putting my stuff on my desk. "How are you feeling? Are you finished sticking your tail between your legs and done licking your wounds after that triumphant performance?"

"Unfortunately, no one's tail was stuck between my legs and certainly no one licked my Axe Wound." I pouted.

Renee grimaced. "Really? We're going that route today?"

"Since nothing was stuck or licked, then yes, we are going that way. Plus, I've got a new kid starting today and I am in no mood to play Mary Poppins."

"If you're Mary Poppins, then I'm the fucking Genie of the Lamp."

"Great! Can I wish for the events of last Friday to disappear?"

"Only if you rub me the right way, baby," she taunted.

"Seriously, I don't think I can ever show my face in Dickies again."

"You've shown more than just your face there in the past. Remember St. Patrick's Day last year? You thought it was Mardi Gras and proceeded to show the entire bar the new bra you'd bought."

"I was getting paid by the company to model the bra."

Renee gave me a *you've got to be kidding me* face.

"Ok, maybe not, but I was very proud of that new bra and I wanted to share my excitement," I tried to defend myself.

I heard my phone vibrate on my desk and I walked over to check who it was.

"It's Martha. She sent me a text." I looked at Renee.

"Does it say that you were really switched at birth and her real stepchild is a doctor's wife somewhere and has a billion dollars?"

I simply shook my head as Renee walked away and the bell rang. My kids came bounding into class and shoved their way over to the carpet.

I looked at the text from Martha.

Martha: Moxie, did you remember to go to your Weight Watchers meeting last night?

I'd told Martha that I'd joined Weight Watchers, to get her off my back about losing weight.

Moxie: I did. They were serving Krispy Kream and I took a stand against their wrongdoings and quit.

"Miss Summers?" Katie yelled, bringing me back to the present. "Can I feed the rabbit?"

Chloe, our class pet, was bouncing in the corner, waiting to be fed. I'd adopted Chloe, the Flemish Giant rabbit, from the Humane Society back in September. I felt bad for Chloe because I truly felt she was meant to be a dog, but got stuck in a rabbit's body. She likes to lay by me and constantly begs for food. She and I have that in common.

Luckily, Chloe is litter trained and can roam free around the room, but has a pen to sleep in at night. I occasionally take her home with me because, honestly, she makes nice company. She's too big for a carrier, so I just walk her on a leash. This provides for some interesting conversation on the train.

"Sure, Katie. Why don't you try selling her some Thin Mints while you're at it?" I said sarcastically, but Katie giggled and ran to feed Chloe. I swear I was going to take her girl scout sash and burn it at night and feed her the ashes.

"Excuse me, Miss Summers?" Mrs. James called as she walked into the class followed by a little boy. "I would like to introduce you and the class to our new school mate, Dillion."

Dillion shyly waved to the class. He was a very cute little boy with floppy brown hair and steel blue eyes. Those eyes hid behind glasses, and just a hint of freckles splattered his nose.

There was something about him that seemed familiar to me. But then again, all the kids blend together at some point.

"Welcome, Dillion. We are so excited that you are here with us. Why don't you hang your things in that empty cubby and sit with us for morning meeting? That way we can introduce you to each student," I said in my most cheerful Mary Poppins voice.

"Thank you, Miss Summers," Dillion spoke in a sweet soft voice.

Suddenly, all hell broke loose. There, before me, stood my Adonis. He had walked right into my room. At first I thought I was hallucinating, like the one and only time I smoked pot and thought that Dave from Dave Matthews Band had snuck into my room. At that moment I decided that I was being punished for all the horrible things I had done in my life. Like mentally hoping that Katie would be crushed by a big box of Caramel Delight cookies.

He looked just as amazing as that night I saw him at Dickies. This time he was wearing khaki cargo pants and a white shirt with the sleeves rolled up to his elbows. Even the hair that grazed his arms was beautiful. I just wanted to lick him like a popsicle.

"Miss Summers, I would like to introduce you to Miles Dane, Dillion's dad."

Holy shit on a shingle. The man I so casually asked if he had hairy balls was standing before me, and his son was in my class. He was probably thinking, "*Shit, now she's going to corrupt my son's education and ask him about hairy balls.*"

28

But instead, all he did was smile. No, it was more like a smirk. A knowing smirk that confirmed he remembered who I was. My stomach started to churn.

"Miss Summers, it's a pleasure to meet you." He shook my hand. The connection was electric, like sticking a fork into an outlet.

"Umm, thank you…"

"Mr. Dane," he confirmed, and then he pulled me in a little and whispered close to my ear. "You know, like a Great Dane. Do you like dogs, Miss Summers?"

No. This was so not happening. My face immediately flushed, but then suddenly I became pissed. This guy had a big set of balls, hairy or not, to have started this game with me.

I straightened my posture to indicate that his presence didn't faze me. I didn't want to give him the satisfaction of knowing he made my Triangle tingle.

"Nice to meet you, Mr. Dane. Actually, I'm more of a pussycat person. I love how soft they feel when you run your hands through their thick, luscious fur," I said, putting a strong emphasis on thick and luscious.

I saw his jaw drop just a hint and then his lips curved up in a smile, so I knew he caught my innuendo. I knew exactly what I wanted to do with those lips, and yes, it did involve running them through my own pussy's fur. I wasn't going to go down that road. His son was in my class and I had a strict rule not to sleep with my students' parents, ever.

"Well, Miss Summers, I thought Mr. Dane could sit in on your class for a while and observe what you do. I'm sure he would love to know what kind of education Dillion is getting," Mrs. James said as she smiled deviously at me.

"Yes, I would love to see Miss Summers teach," Miles said. "Maybe she could teach the kids how to take informative polls."

It was my jaw's turn to drop. I felt my cheeks flame in humiliation. I never was nervous about teaching children. However, with adults in the room, I suddenly felt self-conscious about everything I did. Now, when one of the kids asked me who the 3rd president was, I couldn't fake it and make something up, like Fred Flintstone.

"Mr. Dane, why don't you come and have a seat?" I said.

"I'll be back in a little bit to check in, and then Mr. Dane has some paperwork to fill out," Mrs. James said. "Behave," she whispered to me as she walked out. Glad to know I have her complete support.

"Class, as you can see, we have a new student, Dillion Dane, and Dillion's dad is going to hang out with us a little bit to see what our class is like," I explained.

"Miss Summers?"

I groaned inwardly. "Yes, Katie?"

"We should tell Dillion about the time we went on the school field trip to the apple orchard and your skirt caught on the ladder and ripped off when you fell off."

The kids erupted in laughter and I could see Miles in the back silently chuckling.

"We should tell Dillion the rule that we aren't allowed to talk to you when your blood sugar is low and you are in need of a chocolate pick-me-up," another girl, Annie, jumped in.

"Alright, alright. We don't need to go over past events or class rules with Dillion now. Let's just introduce ourselves and make him feel welcome in the class," I interrupted the laughing.

After our morning meeting, I had the kids work on science centers around the room. I kept my eye on Dillion to see how he was interacting with the other kids. I felt the Great Dane's presence behind me before I could even turn around.

"I like the way you interact with the kids. You're a natural," Miles said.

I turned around to look at him. "Are you saying that I have the maturity level of a five-year-old?" I gazed into his blue eyes, which was probably the wrong move considering the heat I was feeling went straight to my Pussy Cat.

Miles looked at me. "I wonder if he is going to come home asking why his balls don't have hair on them."

I felt myself turn red. "Look, I'm really sorry about the other night. I had a little too much to drink. That's not how I normally act."

"Hmm, that's too bad. Honesty is refreshing." He grinned.

"Well, that's good to know, because honesty has a habit of coming out of my mouth whether I want it to or not."

He stood there and looked at me with hooded eyes. His ocean blue eyes had a sparkle in them. But there was something else there that I couldn't figure out.

"Yes, well, I apparently found your honesty. It's all over my pants and shoes, from Friday night."

I scrunched up my face. "Yeah, sorry about that, too. Can I at least dry clean them for you?"

"Nah, that's ok. I'm just honored that I could partake in the very important bar poll about hairy balls. I can now die a happy man, knowing that I made a difference in the world."

"Hilarious. You won't be laughing so hard when you see my name published in medical journals on the subject of testicles."

Miles's face contorted as he looked down at his leg. Apparently, I wasn't the only one in the room who wanted to hump Miles senseless. So did Chloe.

"Why do you have a dog in the room?" asked Miles, shaking Chloe off his leg and then reaching down to pet her.

"Shhh, don't let her hear you. She's a rabbit, but really thinks she's a dog. I just don't have the heart to tell her otherwise."

"Mr. Dane?" Mrs. James returned to the room. "We have the new student paperwork to fill out for you in the office."

"Great," he replied to her. "Miss Summers, thank you for letting me sit in on your class. I really liked what I saw."

I couldn't help but feel that comment didn't refer to my teaching style. He winked at me as he walked out of the room. Mrs. James followed him out, but not before she turned around to look at me and made a motion like she was squeezing his butt cheeks when he wasn't looking. Fucking cougar!

Chapter Three

After school, I met up with my other best friend, Ryan, at a local coffee shop. Ryan is the most fabulous gay man I've ever met. It might seem cliché for a girl to have a gay guy for a best friend, but if it wasn't for Ryan's powerful Gaydar, I would have made a complete ass out of myself flirting with a guy I had no chance of hooking up with. Some people don't believe Gaydar is real. However, Ryan could possibly make a good living out of it, since he is right ninety nine point nine percent of the time.

He once explained to me that "If a guy is wearing a v-neck cashmere sweater over a button-down shirt and a fedora on his head, he's gay."

"What? That makes no sense. Aren't you stereotyping? If a guy has a nice clothing style, you assume he's gay?"

Sure enough, a guy who was dressed up like an Armani model walked past us and winked at Ryan. I threw my hands up at Ryan in a what-the-hell expression, and he just smiled back at me. Great, I was now doomed to meeting guys who wore track pants and sweat shirts with burger stains on them.

Ryan was adamant about giving me these helpful tips because the first time I met him I tried to get up in his business. His penis business. Ryan is hot. No, not hot, ragging fire, smoking good looking. Someone would have to not have a heartbeat or blood flowing to their genitals not to feel attracted to this man. I even dare asexuals to stand in front of him and not get turned on.

We were at a party on New Year's Eve a few years back and Renee dragged me to her friend's place, promising it would be the event Chicago would be talking about the next morning. It was really six people eating fondue and playing Yahtzee.

"I thought you said this was going to be the ultimate place to be tonight?" I squealed. "And who the fuck still plays Yahtzee? That is such a pussy game. Why not Pictionary, like normal people who draw stick figures with huge junk?"

"It was supposed to be a hemorrhoid, not someone's junk," Renee snarled. "Anyway, there is a guy I've been crushing on who said he was going to be here. I thought New Year's Eve would be the perfect opportunity to get our first kiss, or laid, or whatever."

"Yeah, if you are living in every John Hughes movie in the eighties," I snorted.

"That's blasphemy! Do not speak of Sixteen Candles, Pretty in Pink and Breakfast Club in that way or I will have to wash your mouth out with soap," Renee gasped.

That's when I spotted Ryan and suddenly forgave Renee for dragging me to the Saddest Group of the Month Club Party.

"Excuse me," I told her. "I just found something better to wash my mouth out with."

I casually strolled up to the makeshift bar which was really just crates stacked together with random booze sitting on them. I don't really know what I was expecting here, being these people were fresh out of college. Perhaps I could coin a decorating term called Salvation Army Chic.

Ryan was standing there, pouring himself some Jack and Coke.

"I bet that Coke likes to get Jacked around." I smiled towards him.

Ryan let out a gut-busting laugh. I melted and thought for sure I was a shoe-in to get lucky later.

"I like your outfit," he said. "J. Crew?"

Fuck, this boy was hot and he knew his style. I could tell by his dark faded jeans and cashmere v-neck sweater.

"Good eye," I said. "Mind mixing one of those drinks for me?"

"For a beautiful lady, of course. What's your name, pretty lady?"

"Moxie Summers."

"Moxie? That's an interesting name. I bet that gets a lot of guys' attention." His eyes were smoldering.

At this point I wondered if I should excuse myself to the little girls' room to make sure that my Party Box was primed and ready to go. But instead, Ryan and I sat together on the couch and proceeded to laugh and talk well into the night.

After a few drinks of rum and Coke I was drunk and horny. I was getting frustrated because Ryan wasn't making his move. We had tons in common and I was beginning to wonder if I had rotting corpse drinking breath that was turning him off. I figured he was being shy, so I pulled up my big girl panties and dove right in.

"You know, I'm not wearing any panties and you're making me so wet that the couch will be stained with my essence," I whispered in his ear.

Who uses the word essence? I wanted to smack my forehead with my hand.

"I don't think that's all that hygienic, considering I know this couch's past history. It's seen a lot of action in its past and I can't confirm that it's been tested for STDs."

I laughed. "You are too cute. You're like a little present I want to wrap up and stick in my pocket. Would you like to see the pocket I would want to stick you in?" I said in my most seductive tone.

"I'm sure it's a very nice pocket, but I'm going to have to take a pass," he said.

What the fuck? Who denies a drunk pocket to stuff? I even had gotten freshly waxed to ring in the New Year.

"Oh, but I have a very warm and comfortable pocket with lots of room to move and get comfortable," I tried again.

Ryan looked at me. At least I thought he was looking at me. I really wasn't able to focus. "I'm gay."

"I thought your name was Ryan." I laughed at my little joke. "It's a good thing you didn't give me an orgasm yet. I would have shouted the wrong name," I added with a drunk hiccup.

"No, Moxie, I mean I like dudes."

"Me too! I like dudes who stick their presents into my pocket," I continued.

"Maybe I have to go with the blunt approach with you. I fuck guys, not girls. I like to fuck them in whichever way I can. I like to put my cock in their mouths and come all over their faces. When I'm done with that, I stick my dick in their asses and screw them until they can't see straight."

I stared at him.

"So that means we're not having sex?" I asked.

That's when I passed out. I woke up the next morning in my own bed with one hell of a hangover, and went into the kitchen for some ibuprofen and water. Ryan was asleep on the couch. Apparently, Renee got lucky with her crush at the party and Ryan took me home to nurse me back to reality. We have been friends ever since.

Coming back to the present, I heard Ryan say, "Moxie, do you want your coffee with extra cream?"

"If you're offering me some of your delicious cream to accompany my dark hot liquid, then yes."

"Is everything a sexual innuendo with you?" He smiled.

"Do you believe that Lady Gaga was put on this earth to serve as the gay Messiah?"

"Good point," he said.

We grabbed our drinks and sat at a table in the corner.

"I have a situation at school." I sighed.

"One of your kids slapping you with sexual harassment again?"

"It isn't sexual harassment when you walk into the bathroom in the kindergarten room and a kid is poking at his dingle because it won't go down."

"Well, you are one hot piece of ass." He laughed.

"As much as I appreciate the compliment, I told the kid to pee and the boner disappeared."

"Yes, male genitals are very mysterious in that way. So what happened?"

"I was at Dickies with Renee last week and got a little tipsy. I made a complete ass out of myself in front of a delicious looking guy."

"And how is that different from any other day of the week?"

I shot Ryan my middle finger and he blew me an air kiss.

"The problem is that after I quizzed him about hairy versus smooth balls, he showed up in my classroom today. His son is my new student."

"No question, smooth balls. The last thing you want is to dental floss with pubes after visiting the playground."

"Ryan! Focus. We're talking about me here, not your Pee Wee's Big Adventure going down on a guy."

"Relax, I've seen you drunk and it could be worse."

"I puked on his shirt and shoes."

Ryan howled in laughter. "I take it back, you've pretty much just humiliated yourself into a leper colony."

"Fuck off and thanks, I feel so much better."

"So what did he say when he saw you this morning? Did he offer you an airline sick bag?"

"No, that's the thing. He was smug, cute, hot and completely flirty."

"Horrible. What a fucking bastard. What is he thinking, trying to be flirtatious with you? I'll cut off his balls."

"You aren't helping."

"What's the problem, Moxie? It sounds like you have a hot guy flirting with you even after you regurgitated over his shoes. The guy deserves a congratulatory blow job."

I pictured myself bowing in front of Miles after vomiting and offering to suck him off. I think I just committed myself to nightmares for the next decade. Ryan was not helping me feel better, as I'd suspected when I considered telling him about it. But I still wanted his perspective on it. Even if I didn't like it.

"I think I need to go home and drown myself in vodka and Xanax," I told Ryan.

"Oh, God, don't do that. Then you'll end up all River Phoenix overdosed, with foam coming out of your mouth."

"Well, at least I'll have something white and creamy coming out of my mouth." I smiled.

"Get your shit together and call me later," said Ryan. "I've got a big cock waiting for me when I get home. Tom is back from working in Seattle and we are having dinner and drinks with his parents."

"Ok. Thanks for meeting up with me. Love you."

"Love you too, Moxie girl."

Ryan walked out of the coffee shop. But not before a guy wearing a cashmere v-neck sweater winked at him.

Fucking bastard.

Chapter Four

I had to get my mind off Miles. Maybe if I refer to him as Dillion's dad it will feel more formal. Or maybe I'll say I don't fucking care whose dad he is, I just want to lick him like a Ben and Jerry's Funky Monkey ice cream cone.

I was mentally imagining Miles and putting whipped cream on top of his very large and thick ice cream cone when the phone rang. I glanced at the caller ID. Crap. It was my stepmom, Martha. My mom died when I was nine years old from breast cancer. The memories that I have of her are great ones. She was loving, attentive, and I remember that she loved to do art projects with me. I miss her fiercely and she would have been a perfect person to talk to about the incident with Miles.

About a year after Mom died, Dad went to a singles' mixer at the temple. Martha was there, perched like a vulture, waiting to stick her talons into unsuspecting men. My dad is an exceptional man who is way too trusting. Martha smelled security, both finical and emotional, and went in for the kill.

She didn't have any children when she met Dad and he didn't want any more besides me. Hence, Martha felt that she needed to take over the role of mother figure in my life. Unfortunately for her, I wasn't having any of it.

Her calling was the last thing I wanted. I think I would have rather smothered my naked body in dog food and lay down in a dog park than started that conversation. I do try to like her, but Martha has an image for who she wants me to be and I don't fit that image.

"Hi, Martha."

She hates it that I don't call her Mom.

"Moxie, what took you so long to answer the phone?"

I was waiting to see if I would be struck by lightning.

"Oh, I was just walking in from work," I lied.

"What? At this hour? Moxie, honey, you work way too hard. Teaching kindergarten should be a breeze. What does it take to teach someone to count to ten?"

It's about as hard as it is for me not to hang up this call.

"I've got conferences coming up, Martha, and I was just getting everything in order," I said as I let out a long breath.

"What can you possibly have to say to a kindergartener's parent?" she asked. "Do you tell them that little Jonny is wiping his tushie ok? By the way, did you get that hand sanitizer I told you about from Costco? All those little Bubalas walking around with their germs. You could get typhoid fever or chickenpox."

I groaned.

This is Martha, the doctor. Well, she thinks she's a doctor. I honestly think that she has the delusional concept that she went to Harvard and was awarded an honorary degree in medicine. She quickly tries to diagnose you with whatever aliment she is currently obsessed with. A few weeks ago she told the rest of the family that my aunt had scarlet fever and she was worried that she would become deaf and blind. My aunt only had a cold.

"Martha, I've got good news for you. They now have vaccines for those things."

"Moxie Rachel Lynn Summers. Do not sass me. It is my job to protect you as my one and only daughter. But, I wasn't calling you to lecture you on your sanitary obligations."

Oh, no.

"The other day I was at the grocery store."

Oh, shit.

"And I ran into Diana Goldman."

Fuck.

"You know she's got a boy about your age, David."

The bile started to rise.

"He isn't seeing anyone and she wanted to know if you were still single."

Would anyone notice if I suddenly disappeared to the Antarctic?

"I told her of course you were, because you work too much with the babies to go out on a proper date."

Do they have cookies in the Antarctic?

"So I gave her your number and David is going to call you."

"Martha, you know I'm very capable of getting my own dates."

"Oh, sure you are. That boy you brought to your cousin's wedding was too busy looking at the groom's tushie to know how beautiful you looked in your dress."

"Martha, I told you a long time ago that Ryan was gay and we were good friends."

"Gay, smay. You looked amazing. Even if his Pee Pee doesn't stand at attention for beautiful women, it should have for you in that dress."

"Ok, Martha, have to go now. I think someone is trying to break in and convert me to

Hinduism."

"Moxie…"

I hung up the phone. I needed to escape from reality for a while so I went to my number one escape plan. Tumblr. I've become somewhat of a Tumblr addict, searching for hot men to drool over and images I can become creative about when using my Carl. I booted up my computer and found that I had a few emails waiting for me.

```
To: moxiebun86@ibsglobal.net
From: frenchfrylver@ibsglobal.net
9:26 p.m. CST
Subject: Ryan
```

```
You little wench. Why did you go to coffee
with Ryan without me this afternoon? You
know I need my man-on-man action report for
the week. God, his boyfriend is so hot. Any
chances of me turning him to the dark side
= ) Well, I suppose he thinks being with a
woman is considered a dark side. Fuck!
Princess Mary Weather just scratched my
```

arm! Anyways, I need to head to sleep. I'm
talking to Penis Pauly's parents tomorrow.

XXReneeXX

—————————————

To: frenchfrylver@ibsglobal.net
From: moxiebun86@ibsglobal.net
10:05 p.m. CST
Subject: Tame your pussy

Listen, bitch, I stopped by your room after
school and you weren't there. I had a class
1-A emergency that needed immediate
attention and caffeine. You will not
believe who my new kid's dad is. Hairy
Balls!

Moxie
P.S. – Will you please take that pussy of
yours to get declawed or threaten to
euthanize her.

    I kept scrolling through my emails and ran across an
address I did not recognize. My curiosity peaked and I opened
the message, praying it wasn't a virus or that stupid email that
has you look at a picture for 3 minutes and then the girl from
the Exorcist appears.

To: moxiebun86@ibsglobal.net
From: tennispro4u@sancoequip.com
9:35 p.m. CST
Subject: Hello
Hi Moxie,

My name is David Goldman and I got your
info from my mom, who apparently knows your
mom. I recently moved to Chicago from
Arizona and don't know anyone in the city.
So my mom had to intercede and make a
playdate for me. Let me know if you ever
want to meet up for drinks.

David
David Goldman
Senior Vice President
Sanco Sports Company

Well, scratch my balls and call me Mary. That was certainly
a turn of events. I sat and stared at the computer screen,
wondering if I should respond. When I heard a ding.

To: moxiebun86@ibsglobal.net
From: frenchfrylver@ibsglobal.net
10:15 p.m. CST
Subject: Don't touch my pussy!

It is cruel to declaw a cat and Miss
Princess Mary Weather is flipping her paw
at you. And who has hairy balls? Did you
walk in on one of your students in the
bathroom again? Can't you give your kids
some privacy? Sheesh!

XXReneeXX

———————————

46

```
To: frenchfrylver@ibsglobal.net
From: moxiebun86@ibsglobal.net
10:17 p.m. CST
Subject: Your Angry Pussy
```

Listen, you blonde ho, that cat of yours is an indoor cat. Therefore, she has no use for her front claws except to scratch you and tear apart that butt-ugly couch of yours. And how has your memory slipped so easily in the last few days? Hairy Balls is the guy from Dickies last week. The one I up-chucked all over his shoes? Umm, yeah, him. He just strolled right into my class like it was just another day in Mr. Roger's fucking neighborhood. We can discuss more at lunch tomorrow. Go to sleep and straightjacket that cat!

Moxie

I went back and re-read David's email. He seemed normal. As normal as one can seem from a three sentence email. I was sure he'd keep his sickle-and-blooded-clothes conversation for after he got to know someone. I mulled it over for a while and decided not to email him back tonight. I didn't want to show any desperation. Even if there was some. Plus, I had a date to keep with my vibrator, which I'd just renamed Miles.

The next morning I was in the teachers' lounge getting some coffee. At least that was my intention. I spotted the coffee pot and it looked like someone crapped into the carafe. Mrs. Knolls must have made the coffee again. She was a sweet lady, but when it came to brewing a cup of coffee, she had the skills of a hooker picking up her first John. I was hoping there was enough creamer to make it worth downing. I'd had worse things down my throat.

"Good morning, Miss Summers." Mrs. James walked in.

"Is that what time of day it is? I was more hoping it was 3:05 and school was letting out." I smiled.

"Cute. I had an interesting conversation with Mr. Dane yesterday, after dropping Dillion off in your room. Did you know he is an artist?" She wiggled her eyebrows.

"So, are you going to offer to pose for one of his paintings?" I smirked.

"I would, but I don't think he wants a model who has breastfed three children and whose breasts now point south for the winter."

"Don't be so sure. You can bring the whole Rubenesque women back into popular culture." I grinned.

"Thank you for the flattery, but you're not getting out of morning bus duty. How did Dillion do, his first day? He seemed a little nervous coming in."

"He actually did ok, kept to himself. But who can blame him, when Katie Simmons tries to haggle you into buying gift wrap paper for her girl scout fundraiser?"

"She's going to make a great governor one day."

"Well, she certainly has the scruples for it."

Mrs. James grabbed a cup of shit coffee and headed to her office.

"Good moorrnniinngg!" a high pitched voice squealed.

Amber Smith was a fourth grade teacher and my arch-nemesis at Montgomery Elementary. This was her second year teaching, and from her first day she was the biggest pussy kiss-up I've meet. I honestly believe that she was plotting to take over Mrs. James' reign at the school and turn it into a spa. Her hair was so bleached and dried out that I imagined birds flock around her to try to nest in it. There was no love lost between us, and she was about as fake as her boobs were.

"Moxie, I love your skirt! Did you pick it up at Goodwill?" she snarled.

"Actually, I picked it up off your boyfriend's floor after the great blow-job I gave him. That's probably why it looks familiar," I retorted.

"Do you kiss your mother with that mouth?" she asked in a most disgusted tone.

"No, I don't kiss my mother with it, but I did rim your boyfriend's ass and that's why it's probably so dirty," I smirked.

"You are a disgusting human being. It's really a shame that those students of yours need to suffer through your teaching every day."

"I can't argue with you there, but I'm sure it's better than trying to figure out who did that piss-poor job on your eyebrows."

Amber rolled her eyes and walked out of the door. I'll have to bribe one of my kids to eat a bunch of junk and then puke in her Prada purse. I had some time before class started, so I turned on my computer to check my email.

```
To: moxiebun86@ibsglobal.net
From: ryistheguy@ibsglobal.net
11:32 p.m. CST
Subject: Friday
Hey, Wonder Woman,

Tom and I are having a small shindig at our
place Friday and he is insisting you bring
your mad margarita skills over. Let Renee
know too. I haven't seen her face in
forever.

Smooch,
Ryan
P.S. - Is she still seeing that dickhead,
Bobby? I've got someone I want to set her
up with.
```

```
To: ryistheguy@ibsglobal.net
From: moxiebun86@ibsglobal.net
7:45 a.m. CST
Subject: RE: Friday

Wtf? You have someone to set Renee up with?
Hello? What about your adorable, single,
raging horny friend? Just remember who set
you up with Tom. Me. That's right, not
Renee. And yes, I will bring myself and my
magical margarita skills over. That's
unless something of great importance comes
up and my beauty and brains are required
elsewhere.

Moxie
```

I went back to my inbox and re-read David's email to me from the night before. I decided that I was going to send him my carefree I'm-not-really-interested-but-I-really-am-because-my-Baseball-Mound-is-in-need-of-some-players reply.

```
To: tennispro4u@sancoequip.com
From: moxiebun86@ibsglobal.net
7:52 a.m. CST
Subject: RE: Hello
David,


I'm glad that someone else's mother is as
overbearing as my own. Although Martha is
my stepmom, which makes her meddling ten
times worse, because she's not a blood
relative. First, welcome to Chicago. How
long have you been here? Is there something
special that brought you to the Windy City?
I'm sure it was nice to get away from the
Arizona heat.

Moxie
```

There. That wasn't overcommitted. It had a nice introductory vibe that didn't give too much away and didn't seem like I was overanxious to find out more. I shut my laptop and heard my phone vibrate on my desk. I quickly reached for it.

Renee: OMG I just finished my chat with PP's parents. Apparently, denial isn't just a river in Egypt.
Moxie: First of all, who uses that saying anymore? What did the p's say?

Renee: His parents didn't think there was an issue. Of course they said this as Mr. PP was adjusting his own junk.
Moxie: That's really gross. What are you going to do?
Renee: Put a partition in my room so he has something to stand behind.
Moxie: Good luck with that. Kids are coming in. Talk later.

My kids started to file into the class. Katie came running up to me as soon as she got in the room, with a piece of paper in her hand.

"Hi, Miss Summers. My girl scout troupe is asking for donations to help put pandas back in their natural habitat. Can you donate some money?"

"Katie, aren't there more local organizations that need help, like feeding the homeless or giving clothes to children who are in need?"

Katie looked at me like I'd grown two heads.

"Miss Summers, those things aren't cute!"

"Katie, I don't think it's about being cute, I think it's about the act of giving to those who need it most."

Katie slouched her shoulders and sighed.

"Fine, I'll just tell my mom that you wish panda bears would die."

"Give me the paper, Katie," I groaned.

Katie's smile brightened immediately, like she'd just won a prize at Chucky Cheese. I wondered if she'd need a campaign manager when she started to pimp herself for office.

I was headed to the front of the class when suddenly I stepped on a block from the block center and flew into the air.

I landed straight on my ass and the kids started roaring in laughter and clapping.

"That was quite the performance. I would definitely give it a 10. But the Russian judges might disagree."

I looked up and there was Miles Dane leaning on the doorframe, holding Dillion's hand.

It was finalized. I was going to die from embarrassment. I could just hear the eulogy now.

Friends and family, thank you for coming to the funeral of Moxie Summers. Moxie died tragically from the worst case of embarrassment that has ever been documented. It was her innate ability to make the biggest ass out of herself, especially in front of very attractive men. She will be missed, as we no longer have anyone to point our fingers and laugh at.

I jumped to my feet and straightened out my clothes so I didn't look like I belonged in the morning trash.

"Good morning, Dillion. Mr. Dane, good morning. Is there something I can do for you?"

It tried to speak without my voice shaking, but I was having little success. If he didn't stop looking at me like I was a prime steak dinner I would have to change my panties before class started.

He shot me that award-winning smile. "I just wanted to thank you for helping make Dillion's transition easier."

Crap. He was pulling the whole hot dad and good mannered persona today.

I put on my teacher-of-the-year smile. "You're very welcome. He's a nice addition to the class."

He chuckled softly. "Well, Dillion had nothing but nice things to say about his class. Especially his teacher."

My jaw dropped ever so slightly. If this man did not leave my classroom, my kids would be getting an earlier than expected lesson on sex education.

"That's very sweet. Dillion, why don't you put your stuff in your cubby and get ready for morning meeting?" I said.

Dillion nodded and ran to his cubby.

Miles stood straight and came out of the trance he looked like he was in. "I need to get going. I just wanted to walk Dillion in for his second day. He's still adjusting to everything."

I nodded. "Well, have a pleasant day, Mr. Dane."

"I think now I will." The corner or his mouth curled up and he walked out.

"Miss Summers?" Riley called out. "Seth just said that earthworms look likes penises."

It was going to be a long day.

Chapter Five

Lunch time rolled around and I was relieved that I could finally kick my kids out for some space. I was starting to mentally crack when Austin told the class about his daddy telling his mommy his favorite animal was a one-eyed snake. Then Austin proceeded to ask where one-eyed snakes came from and if he could get one as a pet.

I opened my computer to see if I'd got a response from David yet. I also had a work email set up on my laptop and noticed that I had something in my inbox.

```
To: msummers@d521.org
From: iliketoyap@ibsglobal.net
9:55 a.m. CST
Subject: Classroom Party
Hello Miss Summers,

It's that time of year to plan for our
Spring Into Spring class party. I have some
great ideas and have been talking to the
other parents. We were thinking about
having a nature theme this year. I know my
```

```
girl scouts LOVE to do things outdoors.
I'll let you know when I have more details.


Have a happy day!
Marsha Simmons
```

Like mother, like daughter. Marsha Simmons was the leader in Katie's scout troupe, and equally annoying. To make matters ten times worse, she was also head of the school PTO. She had two other daughters in the school, and only one of them I liked. That was probably because she was a small version of Marilyn Manson and went against everything her mother stood for. I can neither confirm nor deny I saw her trap a roach and eat its head.

Finally, I checked my regular mail. Sure enough, David did write me back.

```
To: moxiebun86@ibsglobal.net
From: tennispro4u@sancoequip.com
9:23 a.m. CST
Subject: Re: Re: Hello
Moxie,


I actually grew up in Chicago and went to
the University of Arizona for school. I
stayed there because I got a job working
for a health club organization. I came back
here when the offer at Sanco Group came up.
I don't know if I would have intentionally
left warm weather and traded it in for
snow. I hear that you're a teacher. What
grade do you teach? I don't think I could
work with kids.
```

```
David
David Goldman
Senior Vice President
Sanco Sports Company
```

Well played, Mr. Goldman. Very suave. He was also playing the non-desperate card. So he worked for a sports company and used to work for a health club organization. I was thinking that he must have a really fit body. I could imagine myself licking up ripped abs and him throwing me around like a sack of flour with his strong arms. Maybe he likes to do it on elliptical machines. All that bouncing could provide one hell of a…

"Hey, did you eat yet?" Renee came strolling in.

"Not yet. I was just reading my email. There is another guy Martha is trying to set me up with."

"Have you lost your fucking mind? Are you purposely trying to put yourself in an asylum? I would just like to let you know that I would not visit you. Remember that guy that ended up in the nut house?"

"Yeah. Didn't you put him there?" I chuckled.

"I was getting confused with all of his multiple personalities. Although, I did like the personality that acted like a horse wanting to be ridden."

Renee and I both laughed at that. We'd both had some interesting participants in our beds in the past.

Renee eyed me. "I think you still take the prize for the most fucked-up sex."

I knew exactly what she was referring to, and it sent shivers down my spine. I had gone out with a guy I'd met at a bar. We actually hit it off great and went to his place after a movie that he let me pick. We started to get down and dirty when he reached for the lube that was in his bathroom medicine cabinet.

Unfortunately, it was nitroglycerin paste, a heart drug that can cause a potentially fatal drop in blood pressure. His dad had left it at his apartment when he was visiting. His roommate found us passed out and naked. After a trip to the ER for fluids and observation, I decided to stock my purse with my own personal lubricant.

"Last time I checked, this wasn't a pissing contest of the worst sexual experiences."

Renee laughed. "Well, that's a good thing, because you'd outrun me by a mile. Let's get back to the real issue. What's the deal with the guy who emailed you?"

"His name is David and he's just moved back to Chicago from Arizona."

"And?"

"And there isn't that much other than that. He's being pretty mysterious," I responded.

"He probably has warts or pustules on his back and he gets off on you popping them," Renee joked.

"Well, so much for eating my lunch." I pushed my lunch away on the desk.

"Miss Summers?"

Renee and I turned our heads to the door to see Dillion standing there with his lunch bag.

"I'll leave you to your visitor," Renee said. She grabbed the rest of her lunch and headed to the vultures in the staff lounge.

"Hi, Dillion. Is there something wrong with your lunch?"

"No, it's just the other kids aren't really talking to me so I asked the lunch lady if I could come back here."

Suddenly, I felt like a momma bear wanting to rip the limbs off the people hurting her baby cub. However, I didn't think the janitor would have appreciated the bloodbath when he was already stuck cleaning the dried-up pee on the urinals.

"Come on in. You can eat with me and we will have a discussion with the class about being welcoming to our new friends."

Dillion came barreling towards me, his floppy brown hair bouncing with every step. He was really a cute kid. But then it wasn't really a surprise, considering the wonderful loins he had come from.

"So, is Chicago different from Maine?" I questioned.

"Yeah. You guys have a lot more automobiles and really tall architecture."

I stared at him, wondering how this kid got the vocabulary of an adult.

"Chicago is known for its architecture. You should tell you dad that you want to go on the architectural tour down the Chicago River."

"Miss Summers, are you married?" Dillion changed subjects. I was taken aback by his question.

"No, not yet," I answered.

"You have a boyfriend?"

"I didn't say that either."

"Well, why not?"

"Dillion, is this the Spanish Inquisition?

"No, Miss Summers. The Spanish Inquisition was in 1478," Dillion retorted.

I suddenly felt that it was Dillion who should have been sitting in my spot as the teacher and I, the student. I didn't even know what the Spanish Inquisition was, just that people use that phrase all the time. I looked at this small child as he ate his lunch that Miles probably put together for him. My heart ached a little, knowing that Dillion didn't have his mom to make his lunches or brush his floppy hair aside when it got into his eyes.

"It must be tough for you to start in a new town and a new school." I looked at Dillion with sympathetic eyes.

"A little, but dad said we can get a dog as soon as we move into our house."

This made me curious. Where the hell were they staying? In a hotel? A half-way house? On the streets? Oh my God. I had to rescue this poor boy from a life of eating out of dumpsters!

I looked at the clock and it was 12:50 and time to pick up the kids from the lunch room.

"Dillion, thank you for joining me for lunch today," I said.

"Thanks, Miss Summers. Dad said you were funny, but I think you're nice to talk to."

If I was enchanted by this young boy, who seemed wise beyond his years, I was certainly screwed when it came to the older and sexy as hell version of him.

Chapter Six

The rest of the week flew by relatively fast. I hadn't responded to David's email yet, still playing the whole who-is-more-mysterious game. I was at my apartment, getting ready for Ryan's get-together, and was waiting for Renee to meet me. We'd agreed on taking the L, as we knew alcohol would be part of the evening's festivities and neither of us wanted to claim the position of designated driver.

It is much more fun to act the crazy drunk ass on the train at three in the morning than take the risk of driving yourself home. One time I was coming home from a date and a guy on the train asked if I had ever seen yellow waterfalls. I knew that, since this guy was stone cold drunk, I would get a fascinating explanation. What I wasn't expecting was him whipping out his dick and peeing on the train's floor.

The outfit I had chosen for this party wasn't overly hoochie, but definitely had an element of it's-ok-to-grab-my-breast-and-do-your-best-motorboat-impression in it. I had chosen my favorite black tunic top and a pair of skinny jeans with black boots. The top sort of had that peasant feel about it, but I wasn't wearing a shell underneath, which turned it into a dirty-farm-girl instead.

I grabbed my purse and went downstairs to wait for Renee. About five minutes later she showed up in a tight mini skirt and a v-neck halter top accompanied by 4-inch fuck-me shoes.

"What the hell are you wearing? I thought we were going to a get-together, not auditioning for Jersey Shore," I said.

"Since Ryan has someone he wants me to meet, I figured I needed to dress up. Is it too much?"

"Umm, I wouldn't say that there is too much anywhere on your body. Plus it's only March. Where the hell is your jacket?"

"What are you, my mother, Moxie? I wanted some cold air to hit me, so when we get to the party my headlights will be at full attention."

I rolled my eyes and shook my head at her.

Renee and I walked to the closest L station. We gathered with all the other Chicago people waiting for the next train to pass. I was looking around the platform when something, or should I say someone, caught my eye.

"Oh, shit," I whispered. Renee heard me and whipped around.

"What's wrong?" she asked.

I knew that balding head as he made his way through the crowd. Joel was aiming straight towards me like a missile finding its target.

"Moxie!" he said.

"Joel." I plastered on a fake smile. "What are you doing here?"

"I was just catching the train back from work. I haven't heard from you. How's your grandma?"

I had to take a moment to think about what the hell he was talking about. Then I remembered the batch of lies I told him to escape his apartment with my coochie and pride intact.

"Oh, she passed away, very sad." I pouted at him.

"Sorry to hear that. Well, maybe now we can get together and have sessions two and three."

He winked at me. Suddenly, I felt the slime that was oozing off him cover my body.

"What the fuck?"

I turned around to Renee.

"Who the hell is this?" she cried.

I looked at her like she'd lost her last wing nut.

"Umm, this is Joel. Joel, this is Renee."

"Joel? So this is the fucktwat you cheated on me with? I thought we already talked about this and you got your dick fantasy out of the way."

I continued looking at Renee, my eyes wide as saucers. It took me a minute until I realized what she was doing. She was rescuing me.

"Right. Oh, sweetie, it meant nothing. I told you that nobody's dick could compare to the warmth of your pussy." I grabbed her ass for added effect.

"So you too are...girlfriends?" Joel questioned as he pointed his finger between us.

"Yes, Renee is my lover. She is a very jealous person." I put my hand by my mouth as if to hide what I was saying from Renee. "But she's a beast in the bedroom."

Joel looked stunned. We all sat there for a brief minute and absorbed Joel's embarrassment.

"Ok, well, I have to get home to um…"

"Sure, of course," I interrupted. "Thanks for letting me try your goods out that night." I smiled and grabbed Renee's ass so hard she let out a yelp.

Joel ran to the other side of the platform to wait for the train. I let go of Renee's ass and turned to her.

"Thank you." I let out a breath.

"Hey, what are friends for if they can't act like a lesbian for you in times of crisis?"

I laughed and saw a homeless man sitting by the wall eyeing us and smiling.

"Sorry, dude. Show's over," I growled. The look of disappointment on his face indicated that our show had been the highlight of his night.

Ryan and Tom lived in an apartment in Lincoln Park. It was very yuppy and I was horribly jealous that they lived so close to the lake. But with Tom being an engineer and Ryan working for NBC as a producer, they could certainly afford it.

Tom opened the door. "My two favorite minxes have just arrived. Now the real party can begin!" He closed us in for a huge hug and a double cheek kiss.

"Were is your worse half?" I asked.

"He's getting some appetizers out of the fridge. Come on in and relax."

Renee and I strolled in. I did a quick scan of the room, but did not recognize any of the faces in there. I walked into the kitchen to see if Ryan needed any help getting the food ready. His head was deep inside their Sub-Zero refrigerator.

"Hey, dildo sucker. Need some help?" I asked.

"Hello to you too, nipple licker."

"I've come to assist in serving your kingdom." I leaned back against the counter, opened the bag of nuts sitting there and popped one in my mouth. I was starving, since I hadn't eaten that much earlier.

"Do you like sucking on my nuts?" Ryan asked with a snicker.

"Best damn nuts in town." I grinned. "So who's this dude that you want to set Renee up with?"

"A guy that is doing some freelance stuff at the station. New to the area. Seemed like her type, without the asshole component."

I helped Ryan carry the appetizers to the living room. People flocked to the food like lions circling around an antelope carcass. I was curious whether Renee's set-up was here yet, so I sought her out in the crowd. I found her chatting up a nice Indian guy with beautiful features. He had dark black hair that was a cross between curly and shaggy, brown eyes and smooth golden skin. I approached the two of them.

"Hey, sorry to interrupt," I said.

"Moxie! This is Raj. Raj, this is my best friend, Moxie. We work at the same school."

"Pleasure to meet you." He grabbed my hand and shook it with a firm grip. He had a British accent, which surprised me.

Not that I was expecting him to be unintelligible, like the guy I talked to when I called for laptop support.

"You as well." I nodded toward him. Can I borrow Renee for a bit? I promise to bring her right back."

"Of course," he said. "I'll just go top off my drink. Can I get anything for you, fine ladies?"

"Oh, we're good," I said. But Renee was looking at him like he was a new shiny car.

"Very well then." He walked to the bar.

"Holy shit," Renee said. "Did you hear that accent? I want to do crazy things with that British tongue."

"Is that the guy that Ryan wants to set you up with?" I asked.

"No. Ryan said he was running late." Renee's eyes were now firmly glued to Raj's ass as he poured himself a drink at the bar.

As if on cue, Ryan approached from behind us.

"Renee," he called out. "This is the man I wanted to introduce you to."

We both turned around and our jaws opened wide, like a baby's when ready to be taken to the nipple.

In front of us, next to Ryan, stood Miles Dane.

"I need a drink," I said abruptly.

I drove through Miles and Ryan and headed towards the bar without looking back. Was it possible that fate hated me enough to send this man into all possible situations I was in?

I reached the bar and found a shot glass hidden beneath the counter. I found the tequila and filled up the shot glass. I took a swig while closing my eyes, wishing that Miles would disappear when I open them. I peeked through one eye and found my wish had not been granted. I took another shot.

"You should probably slow down there," Raj's voice echoed in my ear.

"I was thirsty. Or should I say parched, because that sounds classier?"

Raj let out a quiet laugh. "Something tells me that classy may not be your strong suit."

"I would like to let you know that I won Miss Congeniality for prom court in high school," I lashed at him.

"Don't you mean prom queen?" He glanced at me with knitted eyebrows.

"No. That honor went to Misty Collins. She sucked the entire football team to sway the vote. I would have offered, but I was worried that my braces would draw blood," I confessed.

"Well, as a part of the male community, I thank you for being so considerate of our genitals." Raj tipped his glass up in a salute. "What is your friend Renee's background?" he added.

"Well, she was born in Michigan, she's an Aries and she has one fake tooth."

"Fascinating. But, I'm more curious about her relationship status. Is she seeing anyone?"

I glanced over in Renee's direction. She was talking to Ryan and Miles, but seemed uncomfortable in the conversation, and I knew why. She was the only other one that knew Miles was the man I'd regurgitated on.

I loaded my shot glass with more liquor and looked at Raj. "I don't think she's seeing anyone at the moment. But who knows, that could change as quickly as a baby's diaper."

I took another shot and I could feel my toes starting to tingle. I wanted to sneak out of the apartment, but I had a feeling if I did that, Miles would know I was uncomfortable. His back was turned towards me while he was talking to the others. It gave me a chance to study his ass. It was perfect, perky, nice shape and his jeans molded perfectly to it. He was dressed casually, but in a Sunday football, I won't shower kinda way. His blue button-down shirt was just tight enough to mold to his biceps. It was very nice to look at and I imaged my legs wrapped around those arms as he buried his head in my Pleasantville.

An hour later, I had nursed my anxiety away and replaced it with drunk-girl stupidity.

"Have you seen the size of a horse's cock? I think it's as long as a football field!" I was chatting to, or more like hanging onto, some of Tom and Ryan's friends. They eyed each other, wondering who decided to invite the hot mess to the party.

"That would be so funny, because it has balls. Get it? Football field, balls?" I quickly lost my audience when Renee came up to me.

"Are you ok?" She seemed concerned.

"Fannntttaassttiicc," I slurred out. "Have you gotten to third base with Hairy Balls yet?"

"Moxie, you know that I have no interest in going there. I can't believe that was the guy Ryan wanted to hook me up with. What are the odds?"

"Enough that I would like to go to Vegas. I could make a killing with my luck. What did you two chat about anyways? And why the fuck is he here?" I demanded.

"Apparently, he is doing some graphic design work for the station Ryan's at. He's a graphic designer, but also does other art on the side. Pretty fascinating, actually."

"Whose team are you on?" I exclaimed.

"I didn't know we were doing teams. In that case, I want to be traded to Raj's team. Maybe I can play catcher to his pitching."

"Was that supposed to be a euphemism for catching his spunk in your mouth?" I asked in a hazy voice.

"Something like that. I'm going to go over there and chat with him. His accent makes my panties melt."

Renee walked off to attempt her British invasion. Ryan came up to my side and nudged my hip with his. But because I was a little inebriated, I fell over the corner of the couch and face planted into the cushion.

"You ok there?" he asked.

"Super," I said with my head kissing the cushion. "I was just checking to make sure you sprayed your couch with Fabreeze before the party. I've smelled your ass and it can be quite unpleasant."

Ryan laughed. "So what do think of the set-up?"

"I think you've got impeccable taste, but I also think you lost your contestant on the Love Connection."

"What do you mean?"

"That's Hairy Balls," I slurred.

"We've gone over this. I see a really great chick off Clark and she waxes them clean," he protested.

"No, asshole. Not your balls, and I never want to discuss your balls being waxed again. He's Hairy Balls." I pointed my finger at Miles, who was talking with a group of guys.

"Oh shit, really?"

"No, I'm making this up for my own HBO entertainment. Yes, that's him. The man I questioned about his balls and on whose shoes I spewed."

"Then I take it Renee isn't going to inspect his balls to confirm your assessment," he grinned.

"No. But I do think she wants a taste of Indian tonight." I dragged my eyes in Renee and Raj's direction.

"Hmm, interesting," said Ryan.

"Go, mingle with your people," I said. "Leave me to rot in my own despair and prepare for spinsterhood," I sighed.

"Dramatic much?" Ryan lifted his eyebrow at me.

"I have to make use of the improv classes I took. Besides bluffing an orgasm."

Ryan shook his head. "I need to check if Tom has gone all OCD and is howling at people to use coasters."

I sat on the couch and rested my head back. Forcing my eyes closed, I felt the room start to spin and contemplated what a spinster's life really entailed. Would I sit and spin something on a loom? Or will it be more of an old lady with hundreds of cats scenario? I hate cats and now I was doomed to a life cleaning hairballs and cat poop. Maybe I'll become a hoarder, like on those TV shows, and they'll find cat bones under the dunes of my crap.

"Still trying to impress that Russian judge, I see."

I didn't want to open my eyes because I knew who would be standing in front of me. I could smell his scent, which happened to have taken permanent residence in my nostrils.

"You saw my little mishap, 'm guessing." I pulled myself upright on the couch.

"Is that what it was? I thought you were aiming for a new pummel horse routine."

He sat next to me, putting his arm around the back of the couch. His blue shirt was thin enough that you could still see the defined muscles of his arms. I might have started drooling a bit.

"Do you think cats would eat a dead woman's body if there was nothing else in the house to eat?" I asked.

"That depends," he said.

"On what?"

"On how they feel about cannibalizing another pussy."

My eyes flew open and I looked at Miles. His eyes were burning into me again, like they did in my classroom that one day. He knew he'd caught my attention and I felt the heat in my cheeks rise.

"So you met Renee?"

"Well, sort of. She was with you that night at Dickies, so I wouldn't technically say this was our first meeting," he said.

"True, I guess." I paused, wondering if I should take the conversation further. Heck, why not? I'd already made enough of an ass out of myself. Why stop now?

"You know Ryan wanted to set you guys up?"

"He did mention something about that." Miles took one hand out of his jeans pocket and rubbed his cheek. "But I don't think that's going to work out."

"Oh? Why is that?" My voice came out a little shaky.

"Not my type," he said.

Interesting. I wondered whether I wanted to push my questioning even more. The alcohol in my blood stream gave me some liquid courage to continue my inquiries and advance this little game we seemed to have started.

"And what would be Mr. Dane's type? Enquiring minds want to know."

I could feel the air shift and now the heat that was just in my cheeks spread to the rest of me. He leaned over and put his elbows on his knees, twisting the beer bottle in his hands. I sat up straighter on the couch and looked straight into his rich cobalt blue eyes.

"I like a woman who knows what she wants and isn't afraid to get it. A woman who is honest about who she is, and who doesn't give a fuck whether someone else agrees with her or not. Someone with all the fine features of a woman, curves in all the right spots."

I wondered if I could count the curves in-between my stomach jelly rolls. I would definitely consider it a shape, but I had a feeling that was not what he was talking about.

"Well, it sounds like you have a very specific woman in mind."

"I do," he said, and the corner of his lip curled up.

"So what made you become a teacher?" he shifted the topic.

"I like working with kids, I always have. I got my degree in elementary education and found a job right out of school. I was lucky."

"I know Dillion really likes having you as his teacher."

"Then he doesn't know me very well yet," I joked.

"I wish you were my teacher," he said, grinning.

"Oh, I'm sure I could teach you a thing or two."

"I bet you could." He put his hand on my knee and I knew we weren't talking about elementary education. More like, I want to play doctor with you and show you my boy bits. I felt like I was going to combust when he touched me. I knew I had to change the way the conversation was going, or I was going to be in some serious trouble.

"So art, huh? Do you paint nudes?"

That was not the direction I had intended on.

"I don't paint nudes," he replied. "But I do paint, mostly with acrylics. I also do freelance graphic design work. That's how I got the position at the station. I went to a school for graphic design, but during my studies we had to take a lot of art classes to understand mediums better. Painting just stuck with me. And you can't feed a growing boy on a starving artist's salary."

I started feeling more comfortable talking to Miles. Not only was he easy on the eyes, but he also was interesting to talk to. We talked more about our jobs, likes, dislikes and even got into a heated debate about chocolate chip versus oatmeal raisin.

"Clearly, your views on chocolate chip cookies have been severely tarnished," I tried to say in a serious tone.

"Not when you ingest three packs of Chips Ahoy in two hours, then throw up chocolate chips all night," he laughed.

I suddenly felt a vibration on the couch. Wow, this man had some skills if he could make the couch turn into a massive vibrator. But he reached towards his pocket and pulled out his phone.

He swiped the screen to answer. "Hey, Hon. Right now? Yeah, I'll be right there." He closed the phone and looked at me. "I've gotta run. It was nice running into you again."

He got up from the couch and made his way over to Ryan to say goodbye. Then he ran towards the door and was gone.

Wait, back the fucking truck up. Was he not just flirting with me? He got me all hot and bothered until "Hon" rang and demanded his presence. Well, "Hon" could go ahead and have him. I'll sit here and continue my spinster's life timeline.

Renee bounced up to the couch. "Guess what?"

"Chicken butt," I answered.

"Wait, what?" She looked at me with annoyance. "No, seriously, guess what?"

"What?" I waited, hoping she was going to tell me that they found world peace.

"Raj asked if I wanted to go out to dinner tomorrow night! Isn't that sweet?" she gushed.

"As sweet as stealing some kid's candy and taking a big bite of it right in front of them," I retorted.

"Things didn't go so well with Mr. Balls?" she asked.

"Depends on how you define going well."

"Well, it's one-thirty. Let's say goodbye to everyone and head out," Renee proposed.

"Sure. Maybe if we get lucky we can run into the Golden Shower man in the L." I looked at her with my now glazed eyes.

She reached over and moved the bangs out of my face. "We should be so lucky."

Chapter Seven

The next morning I headed over to the coffee shop for some much needed caffeine. I was hoping that my favorite barista, Josie, was there, because she always sneaks in extra espresso shots in my drinks. Either she's being kind, or she likes watching me act like I'm on speed. I really enjoy the mom and pop coffee house and like to support them instead of a large coffee chain.

I went up to the front of the line and was happy because Josie was in fact working.

"Hey, Moxie. Do you want your normal?" she asked.

"Please. And add some extra love in there, if you don't mind." I looked at the bakery items. "Wait, that chocolate chip scone just threw me a seductive wink. It must know I'm a chocolate whore. Throw it in a bag for me, too."

She smiled and nodded.

"One low fat non-skim macchiato and no whip and three Splenda," called out another barista to the room.

What the hell was that? What happened to plain old coffee with cream and sugar? I was not quite sure coffee had to go and get all exotic. It probably found out that Mr. Coffee found a hot piece of ass in Brazil and suddenly there was competition. I cradled my cup.

"It's ok, coffee, I love you just the way you are. Plus, I hear that the beans in Brazil get one hell of a wax before they get ground," I whispered to my cup.

I had brought my laptop with me to finish up some school work and to catch up on any entertainment news I might have missed. I treat Hollywood entertainment like my holy grail. If a super couple breaks up, I write them a letter and offer couples' counseling. If a celebrity goes to rehab, I start a donation collection at school to send them a fruit basket. When Kirk Cameron went all super freaky religious, I wrote him a letter saying that Jesus left a message on my voice mail and said to tell him to tone it down a notch.

I figured the unrealistic life of celebrities was a way to mentally check out for a while. Like posting an out-to-Lunch-be-back-at-one-fifteen sign on my brain. Plus I really could use some escapism after dealing with Miles's multiple personality disorder.

I was still at a table and opened my laptop to find that I had a few emails.

From: msummers@ibsglobal.net
To: moxiebun86@ibsglobal.net
7:38 a.m. CST
Subject: Are you still Jewish?
Moxie,

I hope you told that person who came to the
door selling you a new religion that you
are a proud young Jewish woman and your
people walked for days in the dessert for
your freedom. Did you get that pimple cream
I sent you? Your blackheads looked very
inflamed last time I saw you. It's because
you're working too hard. If you found a
nice boy to take you out, your skin would
clear up because of happy endorphins. It's
true. I read it in Prevention magazine.

LOVE
Mom

_____

From: moxiebun86@ibsglobal.net
To: msummers@ibsglobal.net
9:53 a.m. CST
Subject: Buddhism
Martha,

I have taken up the ancient religion of
Buddhism. That's because I need peace of
mind, to stop myself from throwing the
computer out the window if you talk about
my pimples one more time. I seriously doubt
that a man taking me to dinner would clear
any acne on my face. If that were the case,
Misty Collins should have had a glowing
complexion for all the boys she blew in
high school.

The Pimple-Faced Princess

_____

```
From: msummers@ibsglobal.net
To: moxiebun86@ibsglobal.net
10:05 a.m. CST
Subject: NOT FUNNY

Moxie, I did not teach you to talk like
that! Your father would have a fit to know
his daughter had a bad mouth. And use that
pimple cream. It was expensive.

LOVE
Mom
```

I folded my arms on the table and started to bang my head against them. Why must my step mother feel I would not be able to function correctly without her interfering? I lifted my head and took another drink of my coffee before I continued with my email. I was starting to think that adding a splash of whisky in my morning coffee was a necessity.

I looked at my inbox and noticed that there still wasn't anything from David. I guess it was my turn to make a move in the game of who can be more aloof.

```
From: moxiebun86@ibsglobal.net
To: tennispro4u@sancoequip.com
10:15 a.m. CST
Subject: Happy Saturday
Hi David,

I hope you're having a nice start to the
weekend.
```
   That might be the lamest opening to an email…ever.

I'm sorry that I haven't gotten back to you
sooner; it's been a crazy week.

*That's a complete lie. I was waiting for you to make another
move so I could save face.*

I suppose you wouldn't come back to the
cold and I bet Arizona has lovely scenery.

*What the fuck? Am I writing an article for Home and Garden
magazine?*

I teach kindergarten at Montgomery
Elementary. I love being a teacher.

*When I'm not contemplating throwing all my kids into hot
boiling water and feeding them to pigs.*

Do you want to meet up for drinks sometime?

*Because I'm desperate to get laid and I'm running out of
batteries for my vibrator.*

Talk soon.

Please email me back soon and put me out of my misery.

Moxie

I closed my laptop and sat back to stare at it like it had
magical emailing powers. I felt my phone buzz in my pocket
and reached for it.

Renee: OMG!!!!! Guess what???

Moxie: They've found an answer to the energy crisis?

Renee: What?

Moxie: Never mind. What's up?

*Renee: Raj texted me this morning and told me that he thought
I looked stunning last night!*

If there was any question whether Raj wanted to get into Renee's panties before, this just solidified it.

Moxie: So are you going to invite his gondola into your river of love?

Renee: We're going out tonight. He wants to take me to Devil's Kitchen.

Moxie: That new place that opened in Wicker Park? I thought it was just a front for a crack house.

Renee: Funny. Gotta figure out what to wear. TTYL!

I was glad someone was going to get some loving tonight. Which reminded me I had to get a replacement head for my vibrator. Since I was stuck being an old maid, I figured having good ways of mechanically pleasuring myself would be essential. I opened my laptop back up to set up my order, but I heard my inbox bell chime. It was a reply from David. I felt a little tingle in my belly.

```
To: moxiebun86@ibsglobal.net
From: tennispro4u@sancoequip.com
10:23 a.m. CST
Subject: Happy Saturday to you


I was starting to wonder if you were ever
going to email me back. My ego was about to
shatter. Yes, meeting for drinks works. Are
you available tonight? I know it's late
notice and you probably have plans.

David
David Goldman
```

Senior Vice President
Sanco Sports Company

I felt like I'd asked out a boy I had a crush on in high school and he said yes. Although I was hoping this went a little bit better than with Evan Harrison in 9th grade. I asked him out and we went to the movies together. Midway through he said he needed to go to the bathroom. The movie ended and I was worried when he hadn't returned to his seat. Then the lights in the theater went on and I saw him in the back, making out with Misty Collins.

```
To: tennispro4u@sancoequip.com
From: moxiebun86@ibsglobal.net
10:30 a.m. CST
Subject: No, happy Saturday to YOU!
David,

The plans that I had for tonight got
cancelled. So does the bar Dickies work for
you? Around 8:30?

Moxie
```

```
To: moxiebun86@ibsglobal.net
From: tennispro4u@sancoequip.com
10:42 a.m. CST
Subject: Saturday night

That time works for me. I will see you
then.

David
```

David Goldman
Senior Vice President
Sanco Sports Company

I let out a deep sigh of happiness. I needed a night out to shake the whole Miles

conundrum out of my head. I couldn't play the conversation that I had with him in my head anymore, or I'd go insane. I still didn't understand why he was so hot one minute and cold the next. Did I accidentally let one rip in my drunken stupor? Renee did tell me that alcohol tends to make me a little gassy. But I didn't think that was the case here. I shook my head to clear out the thoughts. I grabbed my laptop in one hand and my coffee in the other. I had a date tonight and I'd better load up on the pimple cream.

I was in my closet, shifting through my clothing options for tonight. The prospects were not looking so great. Most of my clothes were suited for teaching small children. This meant no skirts, for fear of the kids deciding to play hide and seek and using my skirt as the hiding spot. I also did not have a lot of things that were high quality because chances were that I would end up with tempera paint, dirt, or, more likely, a big blob of snot on my clothes.

In a desperate attempt to find something suitable, I decided that a shopping excursion was needed. And who better to ask for company than my gay best friend with an excellent eye for style. I found my phone and texted Ryan.

Moxie: *Hey, handsome.*
Ryan: *Sounds like you need something.*
Moxie: *I can't call you handsome?*
Ryan: *Moxie, the only terms of endearment you've ever given me are cock sucker and donut puncher.*
Moxie: *Well, I'll remedy that if you go shopping with me.*
Ryan: *So the truth finally comes out. Where shall we meet?*
Moxie: *At the mall. We can grab sushi for lunch and then hit the stores.*
Ryan: *Fine, meet me in 20 minutes. And you're paying for lunch.*

I got to the mall parking lot and looked for a space. I have a small issue when it comes to parking my car. I have this thing that I need to find the closest space possible. It isn't because I'm lazy and don't like to walk. Maybe that's some of it, but I see it as a challenge.

I drove up and down the aisle until I saw someone backing out of the first spot in the next row. I swiftly turned my car around the corner, but there was a BMW waiting for the same spot.

It quickly became a scene from an old Western-style movie. I could have sworn I saw tumbleweed pass by and heard music starting to play. I inched closer, showing the BMW my dominance. Well, I may not have looked all that scary in my Honda Civic. I met the eye of the woman behind the wheel and an idea struck me. All of a sudden, I started flaying my arms around and put on my best sobbing act.

The BMW driver looked at me with wide eyes and backed her car up, finding another space. Ha! The mentally ill woman act got me the space I wanted. My improv teacher would be so proud.

I saw Ryan standing in front of The Sushi Boat, waiting for me. He looked hot in jeans and his tight t-shirt.

"Hey there," he said.

"Hi. Thanks for meeting me. I have a wardrobe emergency," I said as I leaned into his hug.

"You know, Mox, just because I'm gay doesn't mean I have all the secrets of style programmed into my brain."

"You yelled at me for what I was wearing last week and said I belonged on the Wally World website.

"What's Wally World?" he asked.

"Remember, the website that makes fun of what people wear to Wal-Mart. In fact, you pulled up a picture of a woman who looked like she crapped in her pants and told me that was what my jeans looked like."

"Right, now I remember. And I have to say that some of your clothes make people on that site look like Miss Universe," he chuckled.

I flipped him the finger as he linked his arm with mine and we went into the restaurant. I have never been to this Sushi place before, but was told it was fantastic. Besides, I wasn't terribly hungry because I was nervous about that evening.

Ryan and I decided to share a sushi sample platter. He picked up a piece of eel and popped it into his mouth. "So, why the need for the emergency shopping excursion?" He paused. "Does this sushi taste fishy?"

"First off, how would you know what fishy tastes like? You only prefer the pickle," I snickered. "Second, I have a date tonight."

"And who gets the pleasure of your company this evening, may I ask?"

"A guy Martha sorta set me up with."

Ryan was putting another piece of fish into his mouth, but froze. "Martha? I thought we went over this and decided that it was better for you to sell yourself on the streets than to go out on another date set up by Martha."

"We did, but at this rate the Cooch is getting so old that I wouldn't even get a guy off the streets that would be willing to work past the cobwebs of my Bat Cave," I said in a snarky tone.

"Well, we'll pick out something hot that will get this guy cream his pants for you." Ryan winked.

"Lovely," I said in a deadpan voice.

We headed over to Macy's and I pulled a few things off the racks. Ryan was busy talking to the shoe salesman about a pair of Valentinos for men. I saw a cute dress on a mannequin and was about to ask the sales clerk where I could find it when I spotted him.

Miles was at the women's cashiers counter, paying for a purchase. I wanted to hide behind the mannequin so he wouldn't see me, but I didn't get so lucky. As soon as he spotted me, he smiled and walked my way.

Shit, shit, shit. Did I have food in my teeth? Did I put on deodorant? Did I shave my legs? Why would I need to shave my legs?

"Fancy meeting you here," he said, looking insanely delicious in jeans and a white t-shirt.

"Yeah, funny." I plastered a bewildered look on my face. "What are you doing here? I mean, not that you can't be here. I mean, I'm sure you have better places to be besides Macy's. Where's Dillion? I mean, you don't have to tell me where Dillion is. It's not like I'm going to call DCFS on you."

Shut up. Shut up.

He gave me a crooked smile. That smile made me want to jump all over him and smoother him with my jiggly bits.

"I had to get a gift for someone," he said, holding up the bag.

"Well, that's good. I was wondering if you decided to start to cross dress," I said jokingly.

I wanted to crawl into a dark hole and die.

"Can't say that I'm taking that route in life. What brings you here?"

Ryan finished with the shoes and caught up with us.

"Miles! How funny you're here." Ryan smiled at me and I gave him dagger eyes.

Ryan took Miles's hand in a mandatory guy handshake. "I was just asking Moxie what she was shopping for," Miles responded.

"We were just looking for a hot outfit for her date tonight," Ryan said.

Miles's eyes grew wide and his smile diminished at the word date. He turned at looked at me as if I had just stolen his favorite toy. I wondered if I would be convicted of murder if a hanger were to accidentally stab Ryan in the neck and burst an artery.

"Oh, well, don't let me interrupt you guys," Miles said quietly.

"You're not interrupting," Ryan said. "Why don't you join us? We could always use another male opinion."

I was thinking of all the places I could stash Ryan's dead body when Miles interrupted my plotting.

"Sure, I would love to see the things Moxie picked out. I'm sure we can find something to suit her body."

Both Ryan's and my mouth fell open as we looked at Miles. He had definitely put an emphasis on the word body. I moved and grabbed the last dress off the rack, and started walking to the dressing room, feeling mortified.

I was in the cramped little dressing room, looking at all the outfits Ryan had picked out for me to try on. I twisted and turned to look at myself in the mirror thoughtfully with each outfit.

"What are you doing in there?" Ryan exclaimed.

"Hold on. There were a few I didn't like, so I put them back on their hangers," I shouted.

"Screw that," he continued. "Leave them on the floor in a big puddle for the sales people, like the rest of humanity does."

I put on the red dress that I had picked out right before we ran into Miles. I hadn't shown Ryan and Miles any of the outfits that I had tried yet because I was petrified to go out there. I looked at myself one more time in the mirror. I normally wasn't that self-conscious about my weight, but I was a little nervous about what Miles would think. But the dress looked great. It curved around me like it was made exactly for my body. It was sleeveless, with a low cut top that framed my girls perfectly. The material hugged around my hips and my ass in a way that would make J.Lo jealous. I took a deep breath and stepped out of the dressing room. I looked at Ryan first. He had an enormous smile plastered on his face.

"You look smokin'!" he beamed.

I turned to look at Miles, but his lips were in a thin line and his arms were crossed.

"You don't like it?"

"It's fine," he replied.

"Fine?" Ryan screeched. "She is guaranteed to get bonked in that dress!"

I decided that stabbing Ryan in the throat would be too kind of a demise. I glanced at Miles, who for some reason looked like he was going to combust any minute.

"I'll go and pick out a great pair of shoes to go with that dress. Just hang tight," Ryan stated and hurried to the shoe section.

I returned my eyes to Miles.

"What?" I demanded. "Is it totally hideous? Do I have green stuff in my teeth?" I held my hand to my mouth.

Miles got up from his seat and began walking slowly towards me. I started to back up until we both ended up in the small dressing room. I felt the air suddenly get tight. Miles put his hand on my hip and pulled me close to him. I could smell the peppermint on his breath.

"You're right," he said in a low voice. "I don't like the dress."

"Why not?" I asked, thinking I didn't want the answer.

"Because I don't like the idea of anyone else seeing you in this dress."

I was gaping at him. I started to feel self-conscious.

"I suppose that's very nice of you, to save me the embarrassment of people seeing me in this dress. Especially since you think it's as pretty as a hippo's ass."

"I don't want anyone else seeing you in this dress because I don't like the idea of anyone looking at how the dress curves around your sweet ass. Or maybe it's the fact that your tits stand out as if they are offering anyone to touch them."

My jaw dropped down so far, I swear it hit the floor. I couldn't believe he was saying that to me. But then I remembered the previous night, and how he'd turned cold on me when "Hun" called. I felt annoyed. He had no right acting like he was.

"Then I suppose the dress is perfect for what I'm trying to communicate to my date," I said with my jaws clenched.

He lifted his hand and put it into my hair. His blue eyes connected to mine and he was taking deeper breaths, as if to control himself. His phone started to ring.

"Shit," he barked quietly. He grabbed his phone from his pocket and put it to his ear. But he was still looking at me and hadn't let go of my hip. "Yup," he answered. "Fine, I'm on my way."

He let go of my hip and ran his hand through his hair, looking frustrated. All I could do was stand there, feeling beyond irritated. He really had a big set of balls to think he could pull the shit he just had and run back to his "Hun".

"I have to go. Don't wear the dress." And he turned out of the dressing room as Ryan walked back in with a pair of silver heels.

"What the fuck happened there?" Ryan asked, seeming confused.

"Nothing. Absolutely fucking nothing," I retorted. "Give me the shoes. This is definitely the dress."

Chapter Eight

I came home from my shopping nightmare feeling a little queasy. I figured it was a combination of the nerves I had for tonight's date and the little run-in with Miles at the mall. I decided I would rest a while before I had to go out and meet David. I plopped myself on the couch and opened my laptop to check my email messages.

```
To: msummers@d521.org
From: iliketoyap@ibsglobal.org
2:32 p.m. CST
Subject: School celebration
Hello Miss Summers,


After meeting with the other PTO members,
we have decided to do without the
individual classroom celebrations for the
spring. Instead, we are having an all-
school camp-out in which families can come,
set up a tent and sleep under the stars! We
will be having a cook-out, as well as a
fire and s'mores. All teachers are required
to attend. I am sure that the entire school
```

```
will look forward to this wonderful
"adventure". I know that the scouts look
forward to it every time.

Marsha Simmons.
PS. Did you tell Katie that panda bears eat
little children for snacks?
```

I had to take a moment after reading that email. There were two things that were wrong with it. First and foremost, I do not camp. Not only do I not camp, I don't even like being outdoors. I am heavily lobbying for indoor walkways to be built building to building. My idea of camping is vacationing at the Super 8 motel. Chances are, you'll find just as many bugs in the bed there as in the great outdoors.

And I didn't say that pandas eat children as snacks. What I said was that the Chinese eat little girls who forget to wear their girl scout sashes to meetings. Sheesh.

Since I had a little more time before I had to get ready, I thought I'd do some homework. I wanted to know more about David, so I did what any other person would do to gain information: I Googled him.

I typed David Goldman into the Google search bar to see what came up. His name appeared in the first website that was found. It was a Sanco Sports newsletter, the company that David came to Chicago for. I read the small paragraph that welcomed him into the company.

The Sanco Group would like to welcome David Goldman as their new Vice President. David comes to us from Arizona, where he formally worked at Oatis Health Enterprises. David is a graduate of University of Arizona, where he got a dual degree in marketing and finance. David is an avid marathon runner and teaches tennis in his spare time.

I made the mental check list in my head. College educated, check. Goal oriented, check. Physically fit, check. He certainly looked good on paper. I had a little bit of a hard time believing that he hadn't been snatched up already with all these high credentials.

I was beginning to wonder if he had donkey teeth, or reeked of spoiled hummus or something.

I stared at the computer screen for a second. I thought back to earlier, when Miles's hand was around my waist. His hands were firm and big. They were rough, with just enough hair on the knuckles. His arms were thick and his muscles were well defined. I couldn't stop thinking of those blue eyes blazing into me like he wanted to eat me alive.

I typed Miles's name into the Google search bar, curious to see if anything would pop up. I scrolled down the screen. After a few hits I saw his name highlighted, along with the words "Maine" and "Crash". The article was from a newspaper in Maine. I clicked on the link, then scanned the text.

A four-car pile-up occurred due to the harsh weather conditions...

Several people dead...

Wife of Miles Dane...

Child survives crash...

I couldn't continue reading. The thought of Dillion being in that car and witnessing his mother's death tore me into pieces. He was a good kid and no one should ever have to go through that. Now Miles was parenting alone and Dillion would only have little memories left of his mom. I felt somber after reading that, thinking of Miles's and Dillion's faces. That's when the chirp came from my inbox.

```
To: moxiebun86@ibsglobal.com
From: msummers@ibsglobal.com
5:47 p.m. CST
Subject: Date
Moxie honey,

I heard that you were going out with the
Goldman boy tonight. This is incredible
news. Barbara at Mah Jong just asked me if
you were gay. Not that there is anything
wrong with that, of course. Your aunt Irene
had a girlfriend once. She was a lovely
lady until she poured gas on your aunt's
car and blew it up, claiming that she
cheated on her with Uncle Morrie. I hope
you remember to be a lady this evening.
Remember to sit with your legs crossed and
your back straight. I hate it when you
slouch. Curvature of the spine runs in your
family.

XOXOXOXO
Mom
PS. Make sure you were those Spanx I got
you. They suck in that jelly you tend to
have near your stomach.
```

I snapped my laptop shut. I was truly surprised that I had made it into my adulthood without being heavily medicated because of that woman. That thought twisted my stomach even more, but I didn't have time to obsess about it. I had to get ready for the evening.

I entered Dickies feeling slightly better than I had that afternoon. One of the things that helped was that I felt amazing in this dress. Sexy, confident and tucked in all the right places, thanks to the Spanx. I figured if it came down to David and I getting dirty, I would have to sneak into the bathroom to rip the sausage casing off. But this time Martha was right, and it did hide my rolls.

I realized something that could be a problem. I had no fucking idea what David looked like. For all I knew, he could be that toothless hag in the corner eating his bar nuts like it was his last meal.

"Moxie?"

I looked to my left and a handsome man was sitting at the bar. He had dirty blond hair and brown eyes that were so dark it looked like his iris and pupil were one. He was well built, but different than Miles. He seemed to be more toned, instead of bulging with muscles, at least from what I could see over his dark maroon dress shirt. Overall, he wasn't so bad to look at.

"Yes, the last time I checked my driver's license, that was me."

"I'm glad you're not the toothless hag in the corner," the handsome man replied. "I'm David." He reached out his hand.

I shook his hand and noticed the nice firm grip. Yes, you could definitely tell this man was an athlete. "Can I get you something to drink?" he asked.

I was still feeling somewhat queasy from earlier so I decided to just stick with water. When Simon handed us our drinks, he flashed an all-knowing smile. Great! He figured I was on a blind date.

"You look quite stunning in that dress." David's eyes roamed over me. I didn't mind too much that I was being gawked at, since I knew I looked hot in it.

"Oh, this old thing?" I said in my best southern drawl.

"Thanks for meeting me on short notice," he said.

"Oh, well, it was no problem really. The White House Staff thought they would be able to run things without me for a few hours."

David shot me a grin. It was a sweet grin that made him look a little boyish. My stomach started to rumble, but the thought of food seemed unappealing. I did feel a bit more relaxed and I didn't feel nervous about the date anymore.

"So you're a Kindergarten teacher?"

I tried to refocus my mind from my stomach back to David. "Yes, corrupting one child at a time." I threw him a smile. It was starting to feel hot in the bar. Beads of sweat were beginning to gather by my hairline.

"What made you want to become a teacher?"

"In high school I had a male P.E. teacher that would try to get into all of the girls' pants," I answered.

"And how did that make you want to become a teacher?" David looked at me, puzzled.

"I figured that I would become a teacher so I could end up working in the same high school he did. Then offer to play with his balls in the P.E. locker room. But when I went to apply, I found out that he had retired."

"You're very funny. Kindergarten is quite the leap from teaching high schoolers, don't you think?"

"Yes, but I was freshly out of college and it was the only opening they had. Plus, if I didn't get a job soon, my stepmom would have made me work for my Uncle Martin."

"Would that have been so bad?"

"He owns his own fertilizer company. So yes, it would have been a shitty job."

David laughed, but I couldn't really concentrate on it. The room started to spin a little and I could have sworn that David had a twin brother next to him. That, or I was starting to see double.

"So you're liking Chicago so far?" I asked, trying to concentrate on the conversation.

"It's not too bad. There are worse parts of the world."

"Working for Sanco, you must really be into fitness."

"Umm, yeah, you can say that."

It started to seem that he was pulling out the mysterious card again.

"Do you like to play sports or work out?" he asked.

"I do this workout with my fingers where I press the remote until I find a channel that I want to watch," I said, trying to put some humor into a subject that was beginning to make me uncomfortable.

"You should try swimming. It's really easy on the joints."

I wondered why he was trying to push exercise on me, when I decided to change the subject.

"Going to school in Arizona must have been nice," I said as the room was now spinning faster.

"It had its perks. I got to hike a lot. There are beautiful trails in the mountains. It's a great place to ride your bike as well."

David nervously cleared his throat. "You're very pretty. You have, umm, big eyes. I mean they're bight."

I couldn't help but feel like he was trying to come up with a compliment just to make me feel good. He was probably just nervous about the date, like I was. I reached for my water to cool myself down. I glanced up from my glass and saw the door open behind David's shoulder. While I was thankful of the breeze that came in, I was not so thankful for Miles stepping into the bar. He was wearing those same jeans from the other night, the ones that gripped his ass, and a fitted gray shirt.

"Shit," I whispered to myself.

"Excuse me?" said David.

"Fit, I said fit. You seem very fit. I'm sure it's related to your job."

"I play tennis, but not as much as I used to, since coming back to Chicago."

I had no idea what David had just said because I was watching Miles walk in our direction. He stopped right next to David. My heart sped up, and if my stomach hadn't felt like an alien was going to burst out of it, I might have found these two men standing next to each other appealing.

"Moxie, nice to see you," Miles smirked.

"Miles," I said in surprise. "What brings you all the way out to Dickies? I thought you were celebrating a special occasion with a friend of yours."

Miles narrowed his eyes at me as if I was letting a secret out of the bag.

"We celebrated earlier," he quipped. "Sorry for my rude behavior, I'm Miles Dane." Miles snaked his hand out to greet David.

"David Goldman. How do you know Moxie?"

Miles's eyes returned to mine. "My son is in her class, but I ran into her at the mall when she was trying on that dress."

I choked on the glass of water that was in my hand. This dude had a set of balls big enough to fill this bar.

"Well, I certainly am thankful that she decided on that one, because she's beautiful in it," David said to me with wild eyes.

"Really? I think it makes her ass look big," Miles declared.

That's all it took. The bile that had been sitting at the bottom of my stomach leaked up into my throat. I dropped the glass on the floor and stood up to dash the bathroom. But it was too late and I knew I had a problem. I bent over, clutched my knees and introduced my digested food remains to Miles Dane's shoes.

I stood frozen with my hand over my mouth. David's mouth hung open and Miles didn't seemed fazed in the least. I was horrified. I'd just emptied the contents of my stomach not only in front of my date, but also on Miles for the second time. He was going to starting thinking that I have a problem with bulimia. But after that comment he'd just made, Miles deserved a lot more than what had been rotting in my stomach.

"Moxie, are you ok?" David questioned.

"Well, I think that's not the case here," Miles said sarcastically.

"I'll go get some things to clean up. David rubbed my back and headed towards the bathroom.

"I'm taking you home," Miles said as he took a bar napkin and started to wipe the vomit from his shirt.

"The hell you will," I seethed.

"I think it's a safe bet that there won't be a second date, so why don't I just take you home and that asshat can hit up the hag in the corner."

"Here you go." David returned with some paper towels. "I think I should probably take you home." David let out a little sigh and grabbed my things for me.

"I can take her," said Miles. "I know where she lives."

What? This was news to me. Was he stalking me? Would I need to call Dateline and set up an investigation? How the hell did he know where I lived? Oh, God, I hoped he didn't know about my extensive vibrator collection, too. I'd added a new member named Miles Junior. But with the way he was behaving, all my vibrators would have a new name soon, because he didn't deserve my orgasms.

"I certainly don't think that's needed. It wouldn't be very gentlemanly of me if I did not see her home. I'll just get my car from the lot. Meet you up in front. Are you going to be ok until I get back?"

"Yeah, I think so. I'll have Simon refill my water and I'll sip on it while I wait."

David gave me a faint smile and walked out. Miles was still standing in front of me, glaring. Truthfully, I was too humiliated to go home with David, but I'll be damned if I was going to give Miles the satisfaction of taking me anywhere. I sipped on some cold water and took a napkin to blot my forehead. Even though I'd had immediate relief after chucking out my food, I was beginning to feel a little ill again.

"How do you know where I live? Did you sneak a GPS in the dress before you rushed out of the dressing room?" I snarled.

Miles looked pissed.

"No, I asked Ryan for your address so I could come and apologize for acting the way I did at the mall earlier. I shouldn't have run out, but I had something important to take care of." His expression changed from angry to soft. I was starting to become convinced this guy was bipolar. "Ryan said I might find you here if you weren't home."

I'll have to remember to put cyanide in Ryan's coffee the next time we meet. He's such a shit stirrer. It's like he loves to play Days of Our Lives with real people. Next thing I know, my dead relatives will come back or I'll find out I was switched at birth. However, the thought of having another mother didn't sound so bad.

"Well, thanks for the apology. If you'll excuse me, I have to go to the FBI to beg to be put in the witness protection program so David can't find me," I mumbled.

"Moxie…" He grabbed my arm as I walked past him.

"Don't," I whispered quietly. I didn't want to hear anything he had to say. Especially after insulting me in front of David. So I ripped my arm back and headed to the door.

David had his Land Rover waiting for me out front. He got out of the driver's seat and came around to open my door. This only made me feel worse. He was being a perfect gentleman, and all I could do was offer not to vomit in his car.

"I don't always barf on first dates. It's usually more peeing down my leg or my boob popping out of my dress." I looked at him with embarrassment.

"Then it looks like I got the short end of the stick. I could have worked with your boob popping out," he chuckled.

I gave him a small smile and looked toward my feet. "It was nice talking to you for the short time we had. I'm sure it will be a good story to tell your buddies about. Crazy lady spews all over in hopes of being the next exorcist."

"Nah, I wouldn't tell them. But you could give the exorcist a run for her money. And something tells me that it wasn't pea soup that you threw onto that asshole's shoes."

"He really isn't an asshole," I said. "I think he was having a bad day." I remembered how annoyed he'd got in the dressing room when his phone started to ring.

"In my opinion, he's an asshole and apparently blind if he can't see how hot you look in that dress."

I thought back to what Miles'd said about my hot looking butt and my tits sticking out for anyone to grab. The waves of nausea were rising again. "You can just drop me off at the corner. I can walk from there," I said.

"Moxie, I'm not a shmuck who is going to drop you at the corner like a hooker. I want to make sure you get into your apartment ok."

I didn't know how to respond to that. Why on earth would he want to do anything for me after I heaved lunch, breakfast and probably the thirty Kit Kats I ate earlier?

"That's very nice of you," I responded, not wanting to act like an ungrateful bitch.

David found a spot by my apartment building and we both got out of the car. He came around and put his hand on my lower back as if to guide me into the building. It was sweet, and again, I wondered what hidden camera show I was on to be treated this way. We got to my apartment and I dug out the keys for the door.

"I'd like to see you again," he confessed.

"What? Are you a glutton for punishment or do you get off on watching people make an ass out of themselves?"

He laughed. "There is just something about you that I'm attracted to. Vomit and all."

"And here I thought I was the mentally ill one, but I think you get to officially hold that honor. But I'm not kissing you goodnight, unless you want to taste the sushi I had for lunch."

"Umm, I think I'll take a pass on that," he said with a grimace on his face. "I'll get in touch with you in the next few days."

"Great, and thanks again for the water. It was the best 1935 bottle I believe they make. Very rare, I hear."

He laughed and turned to walk back to the elevator bank. When I closed the door behind me, I leaned against it, then slid down to the floor. The wood floor was cool against my balmy skin, so I decided that I was going to spend the night right there. I heard a bing come from my purse, so I grabbed it and took out my phone. It was a text from Ryan.

> Ryan: I just wanted to say I enjoyed lunch so much! I've just experienced it all again in the bathroom, several times.

It was the sushi. Ryan did mention that it smelled odd to him.

> Moxie: Yes, apparently my date got to see everything we had for lunch as well. He was very jealous of the California roll. I thought he might lick it off the floor.
> Ryan: Oh, honey, I'm so sorry.
> Moxie: That wasn't even the best part of the evening. That award goes to me spewing all over Miles again.
> Ryan: What does Miles have to do with it?
> Moxie: He came to the bar looking for me after YOU told him where I live. Said that he wanted to apologize.
> Ryan: I felt bad for the guy.
> Moxie: You wanted to stir the pot, dip shit.
> Ryan: Me??? Never

There was a knock at the door. Had David come back to say that he changed his mind about seeing me again? Or maybe he came back to ask for deodorizer for his car 'cause it smelled like vomit.

Moxie: Gotta go, someone's at the door. I think it's the guys with the straitjackets.

I dragged myself off the comfort of the floor and opened the door. Holy shit, there was Miles, standing there with a bag in his hand.

"Don't you ask who is at your door before you open it?" he chided.

"I figured it was the government coming to tell me that my suspicions that Mel Gibson is really a celestial being were right. What do you have in the bag? Were you planning on playing ding dong ditch and leaving dog shit at my door?"

The corner of his lip tipped up.

"Not exactly. I brought over some Ginger Ale and saltines."

My eyebrows shot up with a stunned expression.

"Why?" I asked.

"I was hoping to save someone else's shoes from being the victim of your wrath."

"Come in." I waved my hand to gesture him in my apartment. "Seems as though I got hit with food poisoning. Ryan has the same thing. Although, if he puked on Tom's Cole Hann shoes, there would be a story in the news about murder."

"Go change into something comfortable. I'll get you a glass of Ginger Ale and you can lay on the couch. Are you still vomiting?" he asked as he headed to my kitchen.

"No, I think I just saved it to be everyone's evening entertainment. At home I just conjure up ways to make myself seem like a complete ass. Wait until you see tomorrow's show," I groaned.

"Where are your glasses?" he asked as he put the groceries on the kitchen counter.

"Third cabinet to the left."

He opened the cabinet and grabbed a glass, then a sleeve of crackers, and came back into the living room. "Do you need help changing?" He smirked. I saw something change in his eyes. Something from compassion to desire.

"Nope, I think I can manage that task on my own." I walked back into my room in a haze, imagining what it would be like for Miles to strip me bare.

Chapter Nine

I threw on a pair of comfy sweats and a concert t-shirt that was old and battered, from high school. The last thing I felt was sexy, and I really didn't give a rat's ass what Miles thought of my outfit. I slipped into the bathroom to brush my teeth. I could still taste the vomit and I didn't want to offend Miles with my death breath. I trudged down the hall and into the living room, where Miles was sitting on my couch, a Ginger Ale waiting in his hand. I sat beside him as he patted his knees in a signal to put my feet on them. He grabbed the Afghan my grandma made for me from the back of the couch and covered me and his legs.

"Thanks for playing nurse," I said. "But don't you have to get home to Dillion?"

"Dillion is at our neighbor's house. He loves being over there because their kids are older and Dillion worships them. I think it's because he's mature beyond his years and they make more sense to him than kids his own age."

"I could see that. He's a smart little boy," I admitted.

"He gets it from his mom. She was also very intelligent, and was able to stay with him at home when he was a baby. I told her it was ok to go back to work after he was born and we'd get a nanny, but she insisted on being with him."

My heart faltered. I envisioned a woman cradling Dillion and singing nursery rhymes.

"I don't know if I would be able to be a stay-at-home mom. I might get a little psychotic. But then again, I work with kindergartners, so I think I jumped on the crazy train a long time ago," I joked.

"She was a great mom," he added. "I just hope I can continue teaching him all the values that she started to introduce to him."

"I'm sure you're doing a fine job of that. He's already turning out to be a strong, confident man, like his daddy."

"Are you calling me strong and confident?" His eyes lit up and he sported a cocky grin.

Oh, shit, I needed to backtrack. The last thing this man needed was an ego boost. But instead I said nothing. He started to massage my feet and ankles over the blanket. It felt amazing and I let out a little sigh.

"So, Moxie, tell me something about you. How does that mind of yours work? I'm sure there are many layers of personality under that sarcasm and wit."

He continued rubbing, but now moved towards my cave as if he was kneading me for information. I really didn't like talking about myself; it always made me feel strange. Although Ryan would argue the point and say that I was my favorite topic of conversation.

"So you noticed the different personalities? Damn, I thought I had them all under control. My medication must need adjustment," I grinned.

I was trying to avert the conversation by cracking jokes. But the way Miles was looking at me told me that he wanted to see my serious personality. I paused for a moment, thinking about the different aspects of my life I didn't mind sharing.

"I was born in Chicago. So I would say I would qualify to be a B.L.D."

"What's a B.L.D?" he questioned.

"Born, lived and died."

"You've never gone anywhere but Chicago? How can you possibly predict this is where you will end up staying in the future?"

"I didn't say that I haven't been anywhere but Chicago. Just that I was born here, lived mainly in the area, and will probably die here. My dad and stepmom live here, and since I'm an only child, my stepmom has now dedicated her entire life to making sure I get married and pump out some kids so she can create a new race of human beings made in her own image," I added sarcastically.

I wanted to change the subject off me. "So, are you happy with the move?"

"I think so. Once we get things settled I would like to move closer to the suburbs, so Dillion can have a backyard to run around."

"And that dog that you promised Dillion," I added.

"Oh, and the dog, of course." He smiled. "I think Dillion misses having the openness we had in Maine."

"I'm sure it was very open, considering about five people live there," I teased.

"You'd be surprised. Portland is pretty big and it attracts lots of tourists. Plus they have a cool art district."

"Yes, I'm sure that's appealing to you, since you're an artist. I, however, stop my creative nature with finger paints."

"Maybe, but you would make a great model."

I blushed a color red that I'm sure Miles could identify on his art palette.

"So your stepmom doesn't believe that you can take care of yourself?" he asked, trying to swing the conversation back into my direction.

"No, I think she's afraid that I'm very happy taking care of myself and I don't need a man to do that." I threw him a wry smile and a wink.

The fire came back to his eyes. "Can you take care of yourself?"

I had a sense that the conversation was about to take a different turn altogether.

"I certainly can. In fact, I like to take care of myself every night before I go to bed. Being a teacher is hard work and I like to treat myself." I wasn't exactly sure when this conversation went from being innocent chat to devious innuendoes.

"And how exactly do you like to treat yourself?" His hands were now moving up to my thighs and massaging them.

"There are several things that I do to unwind," I continued.

"I bet you have a whole regimen you go through. Why don't you share your secrets, because I might want to try them as a nightly routine."

Holy hell. I didn't know if the heat I was feeling was from the conversation or if it was the food poisoning. I couldn't believe that I was heading down this road with him. He was my student's parent. Part of me didn't want to cross that line. The other part of me said fuck it. The second part was in the lead by a long stretch.

"Well, my evening starts out with a nice glass of wine and a soak in the tub. I make sure there are lots of bubbles in the bath because I like the way it feels on my skin." I could tell that divulging my evening routine was making an impact on him, as I could feel something hard under my calves. "Then I get out of the tub and dry myself off, making sure I get all the little crevasses so my skin doesn't dry out."

"We certainly can't have that happen." He took his rough hands and put them inside my pant legs, rubbing them on my skin.

"Then, I slip into my soft sheets, feeling the way they mold to my skin. They're so soft and smooth." By this time his flag was at full mast, straining against my legs.

"Do you wear anything to bed, or do you enjoy the comforts of your bed bare?"

"I don't believe in buying clothes only to sleep in them. In my opinion, it's a waste of money."

"I wholeheartedly agree." His eyes continued to burn.

"When I'm really stressed I treat myself to a massage," I continued.

"But no one is here to massage you," he said, knowing full well that wasn't what I meant.

"I told you, I don't need anyone to take care of me. I'm fully capable of doing it myself."

He stopped rubbing my legs and put them on the floor. I sat up straight on the couch and he knelt in front of me. He put his hands on either side of me on the couch and leaned in close.

"But isn't it more rewarding when there is someone else there to massage you?" he whispered.

"Not when they don't know how to do it correctly. I like a very specific type of massage. It can be hard to master," I retorted.

"I have been known to give great massages." He bent his head towards my neck and started grazing his teeth lightly over my skin. I closed my eyes and leaned my head back, giving him better access.

"In fact, I've had people beg me to give them a massage. They tell me I have magic fingers." He blew air onto my neck, sending chills running down my body and hardening my nipples. The feeling between my legs was starting to become problematic.

He pulled back his head to look at me. He lifted his hand and stroked it against my jaw. His eyes were the color of a dark stormy ocean and I was about to be capsized by them. He started to lower his mouth to mine and I was anticipating what he would taste like. I fantasized his lips were soft and strong, but fierce when he wanted them to be. I put my hand on his chest, slowly moving it down to feel his abs. I counted the muscles as my hand slipped down. This man had a washboard that I could have done my laundry on. I reached his silver belt buckle when I heard a buzzing sound.

Miles closed his eyes tight. I knew that noise was coming from his pocket.

"I can officially say this is the first time I heard *it* make a noise," I said in a sarcastic tone.

He pulled back and reached for his phone in his pocket. He looked at the screen and touched it to answer the call.

"Yeah," he said in a clipped tone. I could tell that it was a woman's voice, but I couldn't hear anything that was being said. Miles's eyes left mine as he sat back on his heels.

"I had to go out for a bit," he said into the phone. "No, I didn't think about that," he continued speaking to the female.

How could I be so stupid? He had another woman calling him as he was trying to get into my pants. I wished I could will myself to vomit on command, because I was starting to feel he needed another dose. I stood up and stepped over him while he still listened on the phone.

"I'm coming home. I'll be there in twenty minutes."

I started to fume as I kicked off the blanket and took my glass of Ginger Ale into the kitchen to throw it down the sink. Miles closed his phone and stood up.

"I have to go," he stated dryly. I didn't say anything, I just stood with my back to him.

"Moxie, there are some things I can't talk about. It's not anything you did."

That was the straw that broke the camel's back. I whipped around, my eyes like daggers.

"Anything I did?" I bit out. "If I remember correctly, you came here to play Mr. Nice Guy Nurse. I didn't ask you to come over. You can take your Ginger Ale and crackers with you as you leave my apartment. I am able to take care of myself and I certainly don't need, nor want, your help." I was pretty sure he understood the message I was trying to send within that statement.

"Keep the crackers and the drink; you might need them later," he said quietly and headed to the door to let himself out.

No goodbye, no feel better, nothing. I took the stack of crackers and threw them at the door. They exploded all over the floor, but I didn't even care. I stood with my fists balled up, feeling frustrated both sexually and mentally. I only had one choice at that point. I had to go and take care of myself.

Chapter Ten

"Who needs a gallon size tub of mayonnaise?" asked Renee, as we cruised down the isle of Costco.

"Well, my grandmother used to make enough tuna salad to feed an army," I said.

"Why does anyone need that much tuna salad?"

"We're Jews, Renee. If we don't have enough food for everyone to eat, plus leftovers, we risk being written into the book of death at Yom Kippur."

"What's that?"

"The one Jewish holiday that all Jews make sure they attend to repent, because if they don't, they get struck by lightning or something."

"So, it's kind of like Easter."

"Sort of. Except without the bunnies and the egg-shaped chocolates."

It had been a week since my date with David and the nightmare of Miles. I hadn't heard from either of them, but I couldn't really act surprised. I was not so optimistic as to think that I would ever hear from David, even though he genuinely seemed like he wanted to attempt a re-do. However, I was avoiding Miles at all costs. He hadn't been in to drop Dillion off at school, for which I was very thankful.

"Will you stop moping?" Renee looked at me like a sad bassett hound with puppy eyes.

"About which part? The part where I showed David the contents of my intestines, or the part were Miles was making his move and got called to the major leagues?"

"I'm sure there was a reason for it."

"Oh, I'm sure there was a reason. It's called he already has a relationship, but is trying to sneak around with the sexy school teacher. Isn't that what all guys fantasize about?"

"Maybe if you were wearing a short plaid skirt, a white blouse tied at your navel and your boobs hanging out."

"Damn, I should have worn that. But it's at the dry cleaners'."

We smiled at each other and I knew that Renee was doing her best to make me feel better. Since she had scored a victory touchdown with Raj, she'd been all hearts and rainbows coming out of her ass. To make matters worse, we were at the store to get supplies for the all-school camp-out that was planned by the devil herself.

"And who came up with the fine idea of a bunch of kids sleeping in tents in the back of the school?" Renee inquired.

"That would be the lovely Marsha Simmons."

I had to put my hostility of sleeping outdoors to the side in order to concentrate on getting the supplies we were assigned to pick up. Five large boxes of gram crackers, thirty bags of marshmallows, and enough Hershey bars to put everyone in a diabetic coma.

Since I live alone, there is certainly no need for me to buy in bulk, but the membership is nice when it comes to getting supplies for my classroom. But there was another reason why being a card-carrying member of Costco had its advantages, and that was the samples.

I take my sampling very seriously. I calculate which way I should rotate around the store in order to hit all major food groups. I usually start by the produce, make my way through the meats, through the refrigerated sections, and finish by the personal heath products. There are magical people in white coats and hairnets that line the aisle, asking you to try their little piece of heaven.

Renee and I were at the start of one of the frozen food aisles when I saw one of my Goddesses offering up some meatballs at the end. I spotted one left on the tray and I started to panic, but I was not too far off. Then, out of nowhere, a woman and her child came up to the sample tray and began to ask the server questions.

No, no, no. This will not happen. I started running like I was trying to beat Jackie Joyner-Kersee in the Olympics. I got up to the post and grabbed the last meatball on the tray.

"Hey, what are you doing? That was going to be for my kid!" the mother screamed.

I bent down and looked the girl in the eye. "How old are you, sweetie?" I asked in my very sweet kindergarten teacher voice.

"I'm five," she responded.

"Well, I'm going to teach you a very important lesson right now that you will be able to use for the rest of your life. You can't always get what you want." And with that, I popped he meatball in my mouth.

The mother started swearing under her breath while dragging her daughter behind her. The Sample Goddess looked at me, wondering if she needed to call security. "What?" I said, still chewing my meatball. Renee grabbed my arm and pulled me away with the cart.

Later that afternoon, Renee and I got back to my place and I was ready to relax a bit. I told Ryan that I would go over to his place tonight and watch Hello Dolly for the thousandth time. I grabbed a drink for Renee and I from the fridge and we sat down on the couch and flipped on the TV.

"Want to watch Grey's from the other night?" she asked.

"Sure," I replied. But, in truth, I didn't even pay attention. I kept thinking about the other night and the time Miles and I spent on this couch trying to introduce our naughty bits to each other.

I didn't understand why he kept running off every time he got a phone call from that woman. Actually, scratch that. If that woman was his girlfriend, I completely understood why he didn't want to get caught. But why would he be here, being so sweet, bringing me Ginger Ale and crackers, if he had someone to be with that night? I heard my cell phone play Girls Just Want to Have Fun (hey, don't judge). It was a number I didn't recognize.

"Hello?" I answered.

"Hey, Moxie, it's David."

The feeling of embarrassment came rushing back to me as soon as he said my name.

"Hi, I...umm, wasn't expecting you to call."

"I was out of town for business this week and was crazy busy."

"Oh, you don't owe me an explanation. I was planning on moving to a remote area were they speak through interpretive dance only anyways."

"Well, I'm sure I could have just asked your stepmom where you were." I could actually hear him smile. "Are you busy?"

"Just got back from Costco with a friend. We're getting ready for an all-school camp-out and apparently they need me to make sure we have enough buns for our hot dogs."

"Well, I'm sure you can provide for some very nice buns." I could hear the innuendo slipping off his tongue. I felt flushed and knew I was going to have to make a stop at the personal hygiene section to see if vibrators came in bulk as well. "Are you available to catch a movie and dinner this weekend?"

I looked at Renee, who'd been eyeing me during this entire conversation. She nodded her head enthusiastically, agreeing to David's plans.

"Sure," I said into the phone. "We have the school camp-out Friday night, so I'll be available on Saturday. Is sometime in the afternoon ok with you?" I asked.

"Great, I'll pick you up then."

"Ok, great." I didn't really know how to end the conversation. Do I say thanks for gracing me with your presence? See ya later, honey? Hasta la vista? So I went with a simple "Bye."

I tapped the phone to close the call and I could see Renee ready to burst at the seams because she wanted to say something.

"What?" I looked at her.

"That was so sweet!" she said in an annoying sing-song voice.

"Someone's paying him off," I said. "I bet Martha wrote out a nice check to him in order for him to take me out."

"Moxie, isn't it possible that someone can genuinely want to be with you?" she retorted.

"Oh, it's possible. But most of them have either broken out of jail, need a safe place to hide their crack, or have temporary amnesia and won't remember who the hell I am in the morning."

"A guy once did that to me," Renee said as she let out a little huff.

"What? Forget who you were in the morning?"

"No, he wanted to hide crack in my place."

"Wow, you really pick the winners, don't you?" I said.

"He said he needed a cool place to put the powder sugar for his mom's cake."

I decided that I had way too much in my own head to try to dissect what the hell Renee's thought process was.

"So did you know that Miles is one of the parent volunteers for the camp-out?" Renee said as if she was making everyday conversation. She knew everything that had gone on in my apartment and how he ran out on me, leaving me feeling like a dog in heat.

"You don't say? Maybe a bear will come and eat his penis right off his body while he sleeps."

"Funny! Your don't look like a bear," she said.

I turned and flipped my middle finger at her and stuck my tongue out.

"I see you've been stealing your students' defensive skills again." She giggled.

"Last thing I want while suffering in the great outdoors is to know that Miles is anywhere on the premises," I said, while picking up a bulk size of Oreos I got from the store.

"You know what they say, don't you?" I looked at Renee. "If you can't beat'm, eat Oreos." And I popped one in my mouth.

Tap, tap, tap.

"Is this thing on?" yelled Mrs. James into the PA system. Everyone in the crowd turned to face the principal, who was standing on a chair. "I would like to thank everyone for coming out and supporting our school for the first annual all-school camp-out."

Excuse me? This is the first? As in, there is going to be a long string of them coming after this one? I might have to consider new employment.

Mrs. James continued. "I would like to thank all the parent volunteers for helping and offering to stay overnight with us. Also, thank you to Mrs. Simmons, who organized this wonderful event for the school. She wanted me to remind everyone that her girl scout troupe will be selling raffle tickets for exceptional prizes."

I turned to Renee, who was helping me set up my tent. "What are the exceptional prizes?" I asked her. "Escorting them to their next Girl Scout Jamboree?"

"No, I think it's a chance to win a My Little Pony party," said Renee.

"But, what happens if a boy wins?"

"Then he gets a My Little Brony party."

We started laughing as Katie Simmons came around with a tray of cookies.

"Hi, Miss Summers. Would you like a cookie?"

"What kind are they?" I questioned her.

"They're the Girl Scout Thanks A Lot cookies."

"Aren't those the ones that no one ever orders?"

"Miss Summers, either you take one or I can pee on it and turn it into a lemonade cookie."

I gawked at her as Renee tried to bite back a laugh and reached for a cookie. Katie skipped away, to ask more people to sell their souls to her.

"So, are you girls having fun?" Mrs. James said as she walked up to us.

"Sure, although I think I would be having a better time if I was trying to rip my hang nail off my big toe," I said to her and smiled like this party was the best thing next to Hostess Cupcakes.

"Listen," she said. "At least I struck a deal and you can sleep in your own tent."

"Yeah, 'cause it wouldn't be creepy sleeping in a tent with my baby doll nightie and my kindergarteners."

"You brought a baby doll nightie?" She eyed me suspiciously.

"Yeah, I thought I could get lucky if Big Foot broke in on the love fest we're having here." My answer was laced with sarcasm. Mrs. James rolled her eyes and walked away.

"I'm sure you're hoping that Miles's Big Foot invades your tent," Renee whispered.

Speaking of the Sasquatch, I saw Miles and Dillion walking in our direction. Our eyes met and I could see the look of regret in them. Maybe he was feeling guilty for leaving his other woman at home while he tried to diddle his digger into my sand box.

"Mrs. Summers!" Dillion came running up to me and threw himself into my arms. I hugged him back and his glasses fell from his nose.

"Oh, gosh, let me get those, sweetie. I'm sure Daddy wouldn't like it if you left them here to get trampled on."

I looked at Miles and I knew he got the real meaning of my statement. I wanted to be mad and keep my grudge, but he was looking so damn sexy. He was in another pair of his ass-hugging jeans paired with a flannel top, untucked. You could see just a little hint of chest hair sticking out of the top of his shirt and his hair was rustled up like he'd just had great sex.

Who knew, maybe before he came, he got some from the woman at home.

"Miss Summers," he said to me in his low, deliciously sexy tone.

Damn him. I wanted to peel his pants down and have my way with him right there. But I highly doubted that was something they wanted to write up in the PTO newsletter. I could see it:

Thank you to everyone who participated in this year's school camp-out. And a large round of applause to Miss Moxie Summers for giving Mr. Miles Dane incredible head for everyone to see. The school now plans on increasing its budget for sex education.

"Miss Summers?" Dillion pulled me out of my demented daydream.

"Yes, Dillion?"

"Did you know that for a butterfly to fly, it must have a body temperature of no less than 86 degrees Fahrenheit or 30 degrees Celsius?"

"That's very fascinating. Where did you learn that?"

"From watching The Magic School Bus. It's a cartoon about a magical bus and science."

"Dillion, why don't you see if Miss Kenny can help you get a hot dog while I talk to Miss Summers?" Miles said as he patted Dillion on his shoulders.

"Yeah, come with me," Renee said. "We'll go find the biggest hot dog there is." She took Dillion's hand and they walked off to the food table.

"Well, thank God for television. At least there is something to augment my lessons of celebrity fashion do's and don'ts," I confided.

"I'm sorry for the other night," Miles abruptly changed the subject.

I looked up to his face. There was sincerity there and his eyes seemed sad.

"You don't have anything to be sorry for," I responded. "Well, except for crashing my date, peeing on my shoes to mark your territory and leaving me sexually frustrated."

"It was you who marked your territory all over my shoes and shirt, if I remember correctly," he grinned. "I didn't want to leave." He was back to a serious tone. "I had something to deal with."

"I'm sure whatever it was, it was very important. It isn't polite to keep people waiting."

He could tell that comment had a double meaning.

"No, I suppose it isn't nice." He took a step closer to me. "In fact, I don't like to keep anyone waiting or wanting for anything."

Oh, here we go again. "Well, I certainly don't like waiting for anything. If I want something, I grab it by the balls."

I heard him suck in a breath. He came even closer, and I was about to fire back another comment when I smelled a rat approaching.

"Mr. Dane! How fabulous that you were able to make it tonight." Amber slithered her way around us. "And Miss Summers, it's nice that you were able to pry yourself away from the food table to help watch the kids."

I was wondering if anyone would notice if Amber accidentally fell over a tent stake and pierced her heart. But I supposed she would need a heart to begin with, and that was something I was sure Amber did not have.

"Miss Smith, this is a great set up you've got here," Miles said.

"Oh, you're so sweet!" She grabbed his right arm with two hands.

"We could really use your help getting the fire ready to roast those marshmallows. We need all the strong arms to lift the firewood."

I mentally stuck my finger down my throat. I could smell Amber's ache for attention, or maybe it was her sad excuse for perfume, Eau de Desperate.

"Sure, no problem." Miles looked at me one last time and left with Amber to set up the firewood.

Renee and Dillion came back from the food table. Dillion's plate was filled with a hot dog covered in ketchup and mustard, potato chips, pretzels, and four giant cookies.

"Dillion, where are you going to put all that food?" I questioned, looking a little skeptical.

"My dad says I'm a human trash compactor," he said with a smile. "I can tell you about the whole digestive system as it goes down."

"I'll let my imagination do that job, thanks."

"Where did my dad go?"

I looked around and saw Miles talking to Amber over by the firewood. He was smiling at her while she busted out her cackle laugh. Then she moved in closer to him and whispered in his ear. I needed to seek security in comfort food.

Dillion pulled on my shirt and I turned my head to look at him. "Would you like one of my cookies?" And he handed one to me off his plate.

"Dillion, did I ever tell you that you are my favorite student?"

His face lit up and he showed me his smile. Some teeth were gone, because the Tooth Fairy had taken them. We sat together on the grass and munched on our treats together.

Chapter Eleven

I couldn't believe I was going to be sleeping in a tent. The only time I'd come close to sleeping in a tent was in 5th grade, when Jordan Swartz and I built a fort in my basement. We turned off the light and used flashlights to make hand puppet shadows on the blanket ceiling. But, when he made a shadow that looked like a large snake, I went running up the stairs, screaming.

Thankfully, I had enough people here to help me pitch a tent because, needless to say, I had no idea what I was doing. Mr. Charmichael came over and offered his services, but when we couldn't find one of the poles, he offered to use his own pole. And I don't mean the one for the actual tent.

Mrs. James agreed that I was allowed my own tent since I did not have any children of my own and there were enough parents for the kindergarten girls' and boys' tents. Renee, however, was not so lucky and had to share a tent with Amber and the fifth grade girls.

I rolled out the sleeping bag that Ryan had let me borrow. He and Tom went camping on occasion. When I found that out, I gave him such hell, and asked if their excursions were anything like Brokeback Mountain. He winked at me and told me that they were better, except without the sheep.

Not knowing what one wears to sleep during camping, I settled for a pair of Lululemon's yoga pants and my favorite cozy sweatshirt. Some might say that my thighs looked like two pigs wrestling under a blanket in these pants, but I didn't care, because I thought they were insanely comfortable, and they made me feel like the other size two bitches who wore them. I heard my phone buzz in my bag and went to grab it. It was a text from David.

David: How's sleeping under the stars?
Moxie: I can't really see them. That might be because I'm
*   looking up at red nylon from the tent.*
David: LOL.

Oh, God, he did not just LOL me. LOL is reserved for sixteen-year-old girls who twirl their hair and chew their gum too loud.

Moxie: Yes, it's a real hoot and hollering time out here.
David: What would you like to do tomorrow?
Moxie: Take a shower to wash my body and my mind of this
*   little outside adventure.*
David: Do you need help?

Hold the horses. Did he just make a sexual suggestion about me showering? I felt a little taken aback, which is strange, because I certainly didn't want to turn down an appealing offer. But something about it didn't sit right.

Moxie: I don't clean and tell on the first date.
David: Well, maybe another time. I know we talked about a movie, but how about a picnic at Millennium Park?
Moxie: Sure, that sounds great. I'll bring some dessert.
David: I don't think I could handle anything sweeter then you, Moxie.

I wanted to ask him if he was smoking crack, but I figured that wouldn't be a very polite text. He was being a little too sickly sweet for my taste. Which says a lot, considering my addiction to sugar.

Moxie: Ok, I'll see you tomorrow.
David: Goodnight.
Moxie: Night.

I lay there, looking at the top of the tent, confused about the exchange that had just occurred. So far, we had only gone on one date, he saw me vomit all over the place, and now he was calling me sweet. I was starting to wonder if someone had paid him any large sum of money to take me out.

"Moxie?" someone whispered.

Oh my God, it's a bear! Or a rabid dog!

"Moxie, it's Miles. Can I come in?"

I immediately thought there might be something wrong with Dillion, so I unzipped the tent flap.

"Is everything ok with Dillion?"

"Yeah, he's fine. He's in the boys' tent with the other dads. Everyone is asleep."

"Shouldn't you be, as well?"

"I couldn't sleep. Can I hang out with you?"

"Umm, sure, I guess."

He came into the cramped tent and resealed the tent flap. I felt a little weary of him being in such close quarters, but then I got a nice whiff of his scent. He smelled like a combination of campfire smoke and man. I thought he should bottle it up and sell it.

"Are you having fun?" he asked.

"If you're calling being strung up from your toenails fun, then yeah, sure."

He let out a small laugh. I loved how his broad shoulders bounced up and down when he laughed. He reminded me so much of Dillion when I said something funny to him in class. I lay down on my side, with my arm and hand propping up my head.

"Not much of an outdoor person, are you?"

"What gave it away?" I snorted.

"Dillion loves having you as his teacher. It makes going to school so much better for him. He feels comfortable with you."

"Why wouldn't he like coming to school?" I questioned. But Miles just looked down at the floor. I took it as a hint that it was something that couldn't be discussed. But then Miles lifted his eyes to me and spoke.

"It was a hard transition for him. A lot to deal with for such a little guy."

"I bet." I didn't want to press further because I really didn't feel it was my place. But I wanted to know more about what was making this man tick. I decided to reroute the conversation.

"Looks like Amber has got her eyes set on you."

Damn, that wasn't the route I was thinking of.

"She seems a little uptight."

"That's putting it mildly. She's attractive. I can see how guys would be drawn to her. But she's like a spider. She'll invite you into her web, then bite off your head for dinner."

He snorted. It was cute, not like a disgusting old man telling a stupid joke kind of snort.

"Maybe. But she certainly isn't someone that would draw me in."

My mouth went dry. "Oh, really?"

He smiled. "I like women who are confident, sexy, and aren't afraid to speak their minds."

"Supposedly Sarah Palin gave up her day job. You could always hike up to Alaska." My voice began to tremble.

"I was thinking more local," he whispered.

"I could see if the art teacher is available. You're into art, right?"

"Moxie?"

"Yeah?"

"Shut the fuck up."

133

He slammed his mouth atop of mine, knocking me over flat on my back. All of the air that was in my lungs left. He caressed my face with both hands and moved his body to hover slightly over mine. His fingers were rough, but still felt like sweet sin on my face. I felt his mouth open and his tongue started pushing at my lips, hoping they will open at his assault. How could I possibly deny the man? I opened my mouth and his tongue instantly slipped inside, curling around my own. I put my hands on his chest and pushed him back to break the kiss. He kept his eyes on me.

"Miles, I don't think this is a good idea," I said.

"Why the hell not?" he asked. He was breathing hard and I could see the pulse throbbing in his neck.

"We're at a school camp-out and we are surrounded by kids sleeping in tents. They're going to think that Big Foot is coming to attack them." And the fact that you're with someone else. But that important piece of information left my mind.

I was also breathing heavily, trying to get myself under control. He brought his face close to mine so our noses started to rub and I started to melt. If he'd asked me to run around the camp naked at this point, I would have done.

"Then you will just have to keep your lips shut while I get you off," he whispered in my ear.

"I don't think the word quiet has ever been used when describing my personality traits." I glanced up at him.

"Then you might want to bite your pillow," he said as his mouth fell back onto mine.

We rolled over the sleeping bag to face each other and I felt his arms reach behind my back. His hands slipped under the back of my sweatshirt to find the clasp of my bra. With a snap of his fingers he was able to release the clasp with one hand. The man had talent.

Yes, I'm wearing a bra to bed. On normal occasions, this wouldn't be the case, but I didn't want to be awoken in the middle of the night, having to flee the camp because of a bear, and everyone see my triple D's bouncing up and down.

After Miles demonstrated his bra clasp trick, he rolled me onto my back. Even though I had the sleeping bag beneath me, I could still feel the rocks from the ground sticking me in the back. He slid my sweatshirt over my head and the front of my bra was still stuck to my body. Miles sat up and drew one strap down at a time, releasing the girls in all their glory.

"Stunning," he breathed.

"Thank you," was all that I could squeak out. I mean, what does one say to a gorgeous man staring at your tits like he's about to have a Thanksgiving feast?

He cupped one breast in each hand and started to rub them, taking each nipple between his rough fingers as he went around. I'd come to find out that this man had large hands: my girls were not tiny tits by any means, and he'd grabbed them like basketballs.

"Tell me, do you like them sucked? Or do you prefer a nice hard pinch?" he asked in a husky tone. He grabbed one nipple with his teeth and pinched the other with his thumb and middle finger.

I tried not to moan, but couldn't help it when a little squeak slipped out of my mouth.

"They will accept any form of attention you decide to bestow upon them," I said in a breathy voice.

He decided to take both nipples between his fingers and pinch, hard. The sensation went straight to my groin and again I let out a little yelp.

"Shhh," he said. "Or I will have to find something big and long to silence you," he said, smiling against my mouth.

I squeezed my mouth shut. Although I liked the idea of him using his something big and long to shut me up.

Miles changed his mind and took a nipple in his mouth while sliding his other hand down my bare abdomen. The trail he left sent shivers up my back. My breath started to come fast in anticipation of what he was going to do next.

Removing his mouth from my nipple, he whispered in my ear, "I wonder what I would find if my hands were to slide into these sexy pants."

A mental note to myself, buy out Lululemon's yoga pants section.

He continued, "Will there be hair covering your pussy or is it nice and smooth? Will it be slick and wet for me or will I have to use my tongue, swirl it around, to get it ready?"

I didn't want to tell him that I was so wet that Noah would have had to build another ark to avoid the flood in my pants. He slid his hand into my pants and into my silk panties. When he reached my hot spot I heard him suck in a breath.

"A combination of hair and smooth. Just the way I like it," he growled softy.

I either had to stop breathing or take my pillow to cover my mouth with, because I wanted to scream out in pleasure.

"So soft and wet. Do you like your clit rubbed or do you want my fingers to fuck you?"

Miles was right, I did have to bite down on the pillow to stop screaming in pleasure.

Miles decided that both options would be a perfect choice. He slipped two fingers in me while he rubbed my clit with his thumb in slow perfect motion. But he quickly picked up the pace. His rotations were going to make me lose it. I squeezed my eyes shut and threw my head back on the pillow. My hips bucked up, trying to meet the pace of his hand.

He scraped his teeth along my jaw and said something into my cheek, just loud enough for me to hear. "When you come, you won't be able to shout my name, but I want you to think it and burn it onto your brain."

I turned my head to bury my mouth into the pillow, biting again onto the fabric so hard I could have ripped it. With his words and the rhythm of his hands I came, hard. I felt dizzy, and when my eyes opened, all I could see was the ceiling of the tent moving. However, I couldn't keep my eyes open for long, and before I knew it, Miles kissed my forehead and I fell into a very deep sleep.

"Mmm Miles, I love playing footies with you, but I don't remember your legs being so hairy," I said in a groggy morning voice.

I lay there with my eyes closed, reveling in the afterglow of a magnificent orgasm. I reached my hand over to touch Miles, but there was nothing but air. I opened my eyes, trying to remember if I'd forgotten to shave my legs. I sat up and looked under the sleeping bag.

Holy shit...

A scream rocked through me as I came face to face with a skunk. When the skunk realized that I was not a cozy place to rest, he turned around, lifted his tail and fucking sprayed me. I started gagging, trying to reach for the flap of the tent.

"Oh my God!" Renee said, as she threw her hand over her face. Mr. Pepe La Pew went scurrying off, knowing that his job was complete. "Holy crap, what happened?" she said, coving her nose and mouth.

I threw my body out of the tent, struggling for fresh air. "No...fucking...idea," I tried to say while gasping for air. Mrs. James came running over, along with several other parents and kids.

"Miss Summers, you stink!" Katie yelled.

The kids started laughing and pointing at me.

"Miss Summers smells like poo," Austin chimed in.

"No, she smells like shit," said Kylie, as her mother sacked her arm and bore holes into her head with her eyes.

"Ok, everyone, back to your tent. We'll make sure this gets cleaned up," Mrs. James said with authority. She turned to me, holding her nose. "Well, I suppose you were due for a raise anyways."

I glanced up at her while I still lay on the ground. "I would like you to know that this gets me off bus duty for life!" I retorted.

She went to check if the skunk had left the area and to see what she could do for me, to ease the smell. Renee looked at me, still with her hand over her mouth and nose. But I could see her eyes, and they were smiling. She was trying her best not to laugh.

"You know, if you were looking for another perfume, we could have gone to Macy's to pick something out that was a little less offensive," she snickered behind her hand. "How did a skunk get into your tent?"

Before I answered her question, I wanted to know where the hell my other nighttime visitor went.

"Where's Miles?"

"Oh, honey, if you think that stink will act as an aphrodisiac, we need to have a serious discussion."

I narrowed my eyes at her. "He was in my tent."

"No, that was a skunk. Unless Miles started radiating new pheromones," she said.

"Earlier, asshole. He was in there earlier," I seethed.

"Miles is gone. He had to take Dillion home."

I hung my head down and rocked it side to side. Why am I not surprised? He escaped before he could reject me face to face. I suppose he liked the little game he was playing. I was never one to feel used before, but at that moment I felt more used then a whore at a brothel. This crap had to stop with him immediately. I could not take another ding dong ditch orgasm edition anymore.

"Why the hell was Miles in your tent?"

"It's something I'd rather not talk about here or while smelling like a horse's ass," I said with my teeth clenched.

"Nope, you definitely smell like skunk, not a horse's ass," she said as she nodded.

"I'm supposed to meet David later."

"Then we'd better get your ass into a tomato bath ASAP."

"I'm not a fucking sandwich," I barked.

Renee couldn't help but laugh. "No, dumb ass. You're supposed to soak in tomato juice when you get sprayed by a skunk."

"Great, so I'll smell like V-8 throughout my date. I can just say, hey, David, did you get your daily intake of vegetables? If not you can just lick me all over."

"There's a come-on for you," she said.

I moaned.

"Come on. I'll go to the store and pick up the tomato juice and meet you at your place. Then you can tell me what the hell happened in that tent."

"Thanks," I said, as I tried to salvage what I could of the camping material.

An hour later I lay in my bathtub, in what seemed to be forty bottles of tomato juice. If I only had celery and some vodka, I could have made a fantastic Bloody Mary. I lay in my tomato haze and thought about last night and what the hell had happened. There was no question that Miles and I shared an attraction to each other. But why did he keep running away? Did it have to do with this mystery woman he talked to on the phone, or was it that he didn't want anyone to know he was attracted to a girl with a little more junk in her trunk? I would have to end this thing.

I then thought about my upcoming date with David. Part of me was slightly embarrassed about going on a date after what had happened last night. But, last time I checked, Miles was MIA, so I needed to move full steam ahead. My baby-making parts were talking.

"Here," Renee barged into the bathroom. "I read that if you mix hydrogen peroxide and vinegar together, that's supposed to get rid of the smell."

"Great, so I'll smell like a salad, between the tomatoes and vinegar. When I'd tell him to eat me, that's not what I had in my mind."

Renee laughed and mixed the solution together. I drained the tomato bath and poured the solution over myself, all while planning the destruction of the skunk species. I rinsed and repeated a few times before I finally came out and dried myself off. I threw on some sweats and a t-shirt, since I didn't have to meet David for a while.

"You smell much better," Renee commented. "Although, now I have a strong urge for a salad."

"You're hilarious. You should quit teaching and become a comedian," I sneered.

"But then you wouldn't have anyone to protect you from crotch-rotting Amber and her masterful plans to destroy you," she said, while batting her eyelashes at me.

"True," I said. "I can use your skinny ass as a shank for protection."

I heard my phone chirp, and it was a text from Ryan.

Ryan: Roses are red, violets are blue. These flowers smell like shit and so do you.

"You told him!" I looked at Renee with exasperation.

"He wanted to know how the overnight went," she said and threw her hands up in a defensive move.

Moxie: Rose are red, violets are blue. I told Renee to fuck off and I'll tell you too.
Ryan: Now is that any way to treat your loving bestie?
Moxie: I don't think you'll feel that way after I give back your sleeping bag.
Ryan: Keep it. Consider it a Hanukkah gift.
Moxie: While I'm thoroughly enjoying this stimulating conversation, I have to get ready for my date.
Ryan: Hope it doesn't stink ;)

I threw my phone onto my bed and walked into my closet, trying to figure out what the hell I was going to wear for this date. I wanted to wear something flirty, but not over the top. What the hell was I talking about? I always went over the top, but the thought of last night's rendezvous had left me feeling confused.

Renee broke my thoughts. "So what are you wearing, hooker?" She followed me into my closet.

"I thought I might borrow your stripper outfit you wore during your days at Lenny's Lounge of Ladies," I smirked.

"Your talent for rebuttals is impressive."

"I think I'll go with a skirt, top and flats," I said as I rifled throughout the clothes. I ended up with a flirty flower print skirt, a t-shirt and a cardigan.

"Aiming for the virginal tactic, I see," Renee snorted.

"After last night's adventures, I could use a little bit of tame in my life. But I am wearing a skirt for easy access."

We both smiled and laughed. I heard another ping on my phone and rolled my eyes, thinking Ryan was going for some more cheap shots. But, when I grabbed the phone, I didn't recognize the number.

"Hello?" I answered.

"We need to talk."

"Who the hell is this?" I actually knew exactly who it was by his voice, but I was playing dumb.

"It's Miles. We need to talk about last night."

"How did you get my number? Are you officially becoming my stalker?"

"I got it from Ryan."

Next time Ryan and I saw each other was going to be his last, because I was going to chop up his body and hide it in little pieces all over the desert.

"We've got nothing to talk about," I huffed.

"The hell we don't. I need to explain…"

"There is nothing to explain. You like to get girls off and run. It's like your own form of ding dong ditch."

"Moxie, that's not what happened." I could hear him getting frustrated.

"I don't have time for this. I have a date and I'm going to be late." What the hell did I just say? Why did I let it slip to Miles that I was going on a date?

"What, with that dickhead from the other night? You've got to be kidding!" he snarled.

"No, if fact I'm not kidding. Maybe he has the balls to finish something you started."

"Moxie, don't." Now I could really hear the irritation in his voice.

"Sorry, can't hear you. The sound of my pussy screaming for a real man is causing phone interference." I knew that was a low blow, but I was pissed.

"Moxie!" I heard him yell as I closed the phone.

I'd had it with Miles's act of leaving me high and dry. It was a bad idea from the start and I needed someone who was going to give me everything I wanted and needed. Primarily, an orgasm without ditching me afterwards.

"Your Rabbi calling you again?" Renee asked, trying to repress a smile. I just flung her a middle finger and continued to get ready.

"Don't you think maybe you should hear him out?"

I spun to look at her. "Are you kidding me? Whose side are you on?"

"I didn't know we were picking teams again, but if that's the case, I pick peanut butter and jelly."

"Don't be stupid," I said. "Everyone knows that peanut butter and fluff is a better option."

Chapter Twelve

I stood looking straight up at a Bean. A giant metal bean that showed me my reflection as I looked right into it. The Cloud was supposed to be an art piece in Chicago's Millennium Park, but quickly became known as The Bean because of its bean-shaped appearance. I looked at all the people passing under its large archway, taking pictures of their own reflections.

"Boo."

I whirled around with my purse in my hand, ready to whip the shit out of the person I thought was trying to mug me, but immediately dropped it when I saw David carrying a grocery bag.

"Down there, Cujo," he said with one hand in front of his chest.

"Sorry, you kind of scared me," I said.

"Well, with you looking as good as you do, I can definitely become lethal," he smiled.

Ok, I gave him one point for attempting to be cute, but minus three points for execution.

"Thanks," I said. "Not looking so bad yourself." And it was true. He was wearing jeans and a navy polo. It screamed prep school boy, but I could definitely appreciate the bulging muscles on his arms.

"Should we pick a spot to set up?" he said as he pointed his thumb behind his shoulder.

"Sure," I replied. We started to walk around the park and found a spot on the grass. David pulled a blanket out of the grocery bag and laid it down for us to sit on. Considering I was wearing a skirt, I tried to figure out the most ladylike position to sit in. I ended up with my bottom on the blanket and legs swung to my side.

David sat and started taking some food out of the bag. Salads, water and a pint of fruit. I smiled politely, but thought of stopping at McDonalds for some real food on the way home.

"I bet eating healthily is part of your routine, working for a sports equipment company and teaching tennis."

"Well, if it was a requirement, then Bob in marketing would have to become bulimic to fit in with the rest of the team," he joked.

But I didn't laugh. Suddenly, I felt self-conscious. Usually, I didn't have an issue with my weight, but something felt uncomfortable about his comment. I looked down and ran a hand over the little roll of my belly.

"So, are you getting to know the city?" I attempted to change subjects.

"Definitely," he said. "The weather here isn't always conducive to going out for a jog whenever you feel like it." He took a big bite of his salad. "What kind of workouts do you like to do?"

I paused before taking a drink of water. Workouts? Who was he kidding? But I figured I should make something up for the sake of conversation. It was getting a little irritated that our conversations somehow revolved around food or working out. With the type of business David was in, it should be expected.

"Jazzercise," I said, thinking quickly.

He laughed. "Jazzercise? I didn't know that was still around. I thought they left that behind with the eighties and leg warmers."

"Oh, no, there's a whole group dedicated to twenty-somethings and they incorporate twerking into the dance routine," I said, sounding very sincere.

"What the hell is twerking?" he asked with a sour look on his face.

So he wasn't attuned to pop culture. I was sure he had other attributes to make up for it. I tried to change subjects again. "So what was life like in Arizona?"

"Fine," he said, looking down to his salad.

"Fine? Just fine? I would imagine that the scenery itself was amazing. I always picture the sun setting behind a cactus and the sky radiating hues of orange and reds."

"Now you're a poet?" he smirked. Something about the conversation was starting to annoy me, but I was sure I was just still feeling irritated with Miles and my nerves were raw. I kept eating my salad, running out of things to say, which for me was quite the feat.

"You have beautiful hair," David said. Ok, now he was trying to play kiss-up. "I'll bet it looks beautiful spread out on a pillow." Oh, shit, he was bringing out the moves. "You and I could get quite the workout together." He winked at me. "I could get those thighs of yours tight and firm in no time."

I stopped chewing and my eyes went wide. Partially because I couldn't believe those words came out of his mouth, but it was what I saw behind his shoulder that threw me into a panic. A few yards away, I saw Miles, Dillion and a beautiful brunette standing by the ice cream cart. The brunette, his other woman. The one he kept going back to when he left me high and dry. What were the chances they would be here? Well, lately luck hadn't been on my side.

"Are you ok?" asked David.

"Yeah, fine. I just saw one of my students."

He turned to look over his shoulder in the direction I was staring. "Isn't that the guy you puked on in the bar when we first went out? Is that his kid with him? I can't stand kids."

I stopped to look at him, wondering what the hell I was doing sitting there with a guy who made comments about my thighs and his hatred of kids. I was a teacher, for Christ's sake. David's dating score was sinking by the second.

Not a minute later, Dillion spotted me. "Miss Summers!" he screamed. He broke his hand away from Miles and came shooting towards me like a missile. No, no, no. I wanted to yell at him to heel, sit and stay like a dog, so I could hightail it out of there. But it was too late. He flew at me with a hug that knocked me over.

"Miss Summers, what are you doing here? Did you know I was going to be here too?

Did you know that the St. Louis Arch is six hundred and thirty feet tall? And did you know that it was designed by Finnish-American architect Eero Saarinen and German-American structural engineer Hannskarl Bandel?"

"Excuse me, how old is this kid?" David looked at me as I was trying to reseat myself on the blanket.

"He's in my class," I answered.

I turned to Dillion. "Dillion, I'm out with my friend, Mr. Goldman."

"Is he your boyfriend?" I looked at him as if he'd just asked me if I'd had my annual pap.

"Dillion, your ice cream is melting," I heard Miles as he approached our blanket.

"But Dad, Miss Summers is here with her boyfriend."

I froze and looked directly at Miles. I was still angry about the night before, so I scooted next to David and put my hand on his thigh. Miles turned a shade of red that I don't believe had a name in the Crayola box.

"Miss Summers," Miles said through gritted teeth.

"Mr. Dane. I hope you're enjoying this wonderful afternoon with your family." My eyes darted to the brunette still by the ice cream cart. "I'm sure it's nice to be with them after your busy night at the school camp-out," I said with one of my brows arched.

"Actually, I didn't get much sleep at the camp-out. I was pretty distracted for most of the evening." His face color returned to normal. Now he knew I was playing a game with him. But there was no way I was going to give him the upper hand. I nuzzled in close into David's neck, surprising both men.

"Daddy?"

We all looked at Dillion, who started to look a little pale.

"Kid, if you're going to throw up, aim that way," David said as he pointed to Miles.

Miles ran to Dillion's side and bent down to whisper something into his ear. Dillion started shaking and a blank glaze took over his eyes. I released David's thigh and stood up to get to Dillion, but before I could reach them Miles picked Dillion up in his arms and started walking back to the brunette. I was speechless. I couldn't call after him because I didn't know what to say or if it was my place to say anything at all.

"Weird kid," I heard David say behind my back.

"He's actually a very sweet kid who has been though a lot," I snapped unintentionally.

"Whoa, down there, tiger," he said. "Kids just freak me out a little. Why don't we go back to my place and pick out a movie to watch?"

I wasn't really thinking when I responded. I just nodded my head and kept looking in the direction Miles and Dillion were headed. I couldn't get rid of the aching feeling that something was wrong. David packed up the picnic and grabbed my hand to start walking.

We walked to David's high-rise apartment, which wasn't too far from the park. I still felt a little unsettled about what had happened to Dillion, but I tried to put it out of my head, thinking it was none of my business. The building David lived in was modern with a hint of stuffiness. Something I definitely was not used to. He gave the doorman a nod of his head and we entered the elevator to go up to his apartment.

"This is a really nice place," I said.

"You haven't even seen my place yet," he laughed.

"I'm sure it's nice, too."

"Well, don't you want to come see for yourself?"

He opened the door to the apartment and I had to pick up my jaw that had hit the floor. The foyer lead straight into the living room, which was furnished with modern décor. Off to the left was a kitchen which had granite countertops and stainless steel appliances.

"You're right," I said. "The rest of the place is trashy compared to your apartment."

He chuckled and put down the bag he was carrying. He came up behind me and put his hands on my arms. He slowly started moving them up and down and bent his neck to whisper in my ear. "You know, I can help you tone up your arms."

I really wasn't on the same page as he was, and my head was definitely in another universe altogether.

"You jacking me off will give your arms a good workout."

Then he spun me around to face him and smashed his mouth onto mine. I stood there, not understanding what the hell had just happened. His mouth was everywhere. I even think he put his tongue in my nose. He pulled his mouth free from me and rubbed his erection up against my thigh.

"You know, if we put you on a meal plan and workout with a trainer three times a week, you can get fit in no time. I bet you have a sexy woman under all of that," he said.

I took my hands and pushed his chest so he went flying a few feet backwards.

"What did you say?" I said quietly.

"It's not healthy to carry all that extra weight around. I can help you trim up and you'll feel much better about yourself. I really think that your body has great potential."

I was blown away. I couldn't even come up with a witty remark because I felt too insulted and humiliated.

"Why, then?" I asked.

"Why what?"

"If you think I'm such a fucking whale, why did you even ask me out?" At this point I had raised my voice a couple of notches above normal. "What, is this the test drive Free Willy to get your rocks off?"

David stood there with his hands on his hips and a look of irritation on his face.

"Well?" I screamed.

"My company has a new diet plan that they want to start rolling out next year. We need people to try out the program so we can get some testimonials for when the product launches. When our moms met in the store that day, your mom thought you might be a good candidate, but she thought that me asking you directly would have seemed too crass. So she asked me to take you out and get to know you before I asked you to do it."

I didn't know what to process first. The fact that Martha basically set me up with a guy to help me lose weight, or the fact that I was about to castrate this man standing before me? I went with the latter. I strolled up to him with grace and placed both hands on his chest. I looked up at him through my eyelashes and pulled out my sweetest smile. Then I turned my head to whisper into his ear.

"It's a good thing you don't like children," I said sweetly. Then I lifted my knee with everything I had, straight into his crotch. He grabbed his balls and went straight to his knees, crying in pain. "Because you don't have the balls to be a decent man." I grabbed my purse and ran out of there, leaving David bent over in the same misery I was feeling.

Chapter Thirteen

I sat there, in my apartment, with my friend Jack. Jack is a good listener and he likes to soothe me. The best part about Jack is he never talks back. I poured the rest of the Jack that I had into the Coke in my cup and drank it all down in one swoop. It had been two days since the incident with David and I'd held myself prisoner in my apartment. I even took a sick day because I couldn't stand the thought of me dragging my fat ass to work.

I hadn't even bothered brushing my hair or my teeth for the last two days. There were pizza boxes and empty ice cream cartons spread across the floor. Yes, I was in the middle of a pity party, and I was the host of the evening. Both Ryan and Renee had tried calling me, but I had let everything go to voicemail because I wasn't in the mood for the pep talk. I did however manage to write an email to Martha, expressing my thoughts about her little arrangement she had put me in.

```
From: moxiebun86@ibsglobal.net
To: msummers@ibsglobal.net
10:53 p.m. CST
Subject: Fat farm
Dear Mommy Dearest,

You'll be pleased to know that I have flown
away to join a community of people that can
accept me for who I am. A wonderful group
of people with luscious rolls of fat
seeping from their bodies. I've become best
friends with a girl who has multiple chins
and can hide pieces of food in there for us
to snack on later. They provide wonderful
activities including the Jelly Roll Jiggle,
where we all slather jelly on our stomachs
and smash into each other like in a mosh
pit. My personal favorite pastime is the
Hog's Heaven Spa, where we all sit in a
bunch of shit talking about how fat as pigs
we are. Please do not come looking for me,
as you will not be able to trace my steps.
Unless you find the crumbs of the
Snickerdoodle cookies I was eating on my
way here.

Sincerely,
Your fabulously fat stepdaughter.
```

Ok, so it was a little over the top. But I think it got the point across to her that I was pissed to say the least. I turned on the television and became engrossed in the show "I Gave Birth and Never Knew I was Pregnant." Then I was a little concerned that I could very well have a baby growing inside of me and not know it. There was a knock at the door that broke my thoughts of giving birth on my couch. I opened the door and there stood Miles.

"Still have a problem asking who's at the door before answering, I see."

"What do you want? I have company," I slurred.

"Oh, yeah? Is it that winner from the park the other day?" he asked as he put both hands on the door frame.

"No, I have a date with Jack. He's super hot and is a good quick fuck," I sneered.

"You must have given him one hell of a blow job because I can smell him all over your breath."

"Fuck you," I said and turned to walk back into my apartment.

"Tempting," he said. "But not why I came here."

"Oh, so you came here to get me hot and bothered, get me off, laugh at the fat girl and ditch me behind. Sorry, that game has already been played."

"Wait, what did you say?" I could hear his breathing become rough, like he was pissed.

"I said, that game has already been played. David tried to get into my big girl panties so he could see if he could get me to drop the weight and be his model for his slim-trim company. Apparently, my fat ass could have been his model."

Miles took three long strides to get behind me. He grabbed my hips and spun me around. Then he moved his hands to my face and braced my cheeks.

"I don't want to ever hear you talk about yourself that way again. Do you understand me?" he said with a strained voice.

"And why the fuck do you care? You go home to a beautiful skinny brunette every night. What? Does she not have enough junk in her trunk to hold onto when you screw her?"

He looked me straight in the eyes. I could see the dark blue pools of his irises radiate through me.

"I mean it, Moxie. You don't know what the hell you're talking about and you're too drunk for me to explain any of it."

"Well, then it should be easy for you. Screw the fatty and then leave to go back to your happy little home."

"Moxie, it is taking everything inside me not to kiss that filthy mouth of yours. But you need to listen to me explain everything and I can't do it with you like this," he said calmly.

"So what are you going to do about it? Sit on the damn stoop until the morning?" I snarled.

"No, I'm going to strip you down, get you in the shower, because, frankly, you reek of Jack and Coke, then I'm going to put you to bed."

He lifted me off the ground and threw me over his shoulder. I let out a yelp of surprise as he walked me into the bathroom. He turned on the shower and set me down on the vanity. He stuck his hand in to feel the temperature of the water and when he deemed it comfortable he turned back to me. He grabbed the hem of my shirt and gently pulled it over my head. I hadn't even bothered putting a bra on the past two days, so my breasts were fully exposed.

He took my hips and glided me off the counter so I was standing up. Slowly, he tapped each ankle for me to lift my foot so he could remove my socks. He stood upright and sank his fingers into my sweat pants, and started to pull them down.

I grabbed his hands in order for him to stop. But then he looked at me, and suddenly I felt safe. He pulled down my pants, along with my panties, and gazed back up to met my eyes. I felt the most vulnerable I ever had at that moment.

"Ready to get wet?" he finally spoke.

"I think I was already there when you came into my apartment," I said in a breathy voice.

He smiled and took my hand. He slid the shower curtain to the side and helped me into the tub. The water was perfect, warm and calming. I hadn't expected what happened next. Miles reached for the back of his collar and lifted his shirt above his head. It was the first time I saw his broad chest and the dark hair covering it. The hair trailed past his navel and disappeared under his jeans. He unfastened his belt and my body began to shake, partly because of the cold air contrasting with the warm water, partly because I wanted to see what was under his jeans.

His jeans fell to the floor and my Adonis stood there, looking sexy as hell in his boxer briefs. I suddenly felt conscious of my body, looking at this man that was made of pure muscle. I tried to use my hands to cover up my body, but when I did, Miles grabbed my wrists and brought them to my sides.

"Don't ever cover yourself in front of me," he said in a husky tone.

All I could do was nod, and he stepped in the tub with me. "Your boxers are getting wet," I said, as I blatantly stared at his erection.

"I'm trying my best to be somewhat of a gentleman. If I lose the boxers, I'll also lose my self-control. All I want to do is wash you down, sober you up a little, and put you to bed."

"But then you'll leave and go back to her," I said, a little more harshly then I meant to.

"I told you that we'd talk about it. But I won't do it until your head is clear. Now pass me the soap so I can shampoo your hair."

It was one of the most intimate acts I've ever partaken in. Miles ran his fingers through my hair, massaging the scalp with the shampoo. I stood with my body facing the shower head, letting the water run down my front, warming me and taking my stress down the drain.

"What the hell is this?" Miles asked.

I turned my head to see what he was talking about. "It's a poof," I said with a smile.

"A what?"

"You know, a poof."

"Is it some kind of sex toy?" he teased.

I grabbed the poof out of his hand and put some soap into it, lathered it up and handed it back to Miles.

"Isn't this why they make washcloths?" I could hear the smile in his voice.

"You have thirty seconds to loofa my ass or I'm kicking you out of the shower," I demanded.

"Yes, Ma'am!"

When Miles was done rinsing me off, he turned off the shower and opened the curtain. He grabbed a towel off the drying rack and wiped me dry, staying a little longer on my breasts to make sure they were thoroughly dried. He took the second towel and wrapped it around his waist. Miles lifted me out of the tub, cradled me into his arms and walked us back into my bedroom. He pulled the covers off and I didn't even bother putting some pajamas on. The sheets felt comfortable on my skin, like laying on a soft cloud.

"I promise we'll talk," he whispered as he smoothed my hair off my forehead. Then he bent down to give me a kiss on the cheek. I don't remember what happened after that because I feel into deep, peaceful sleep.

A bunch of girls were trampling over my head to get over to the boy band that was playing. I opened my eyes and realized that no girls were smashing my head and the alarm was blasting Back Street Boys. The feeling I had in my head was a hangover from hell. My friend Jack was now officially disowned.

I reached my hand over to shut off the alarm, when I quickly realized that it was Tuesday and I needed to get ready for work. I wondered what would happen if I quit today and lived off the land. Then again, I didn't believe that the land provided Prada handbags.

I walked into my closet to find something that was work suitable, but also comfortable. The last thing I wanted was a pair of Spanx trying to squeeze the remaining alcohol out of my body. I decided to go with gray slacks with an elastic waistband and a black long tunic, to hide the fact that I was wearing pants only seen on little old ladies.

Glancing into my refrigerator, I found nothing that seemed remotely appetizing for breakfast. I had a feeling that anything I ended up eating would be revisited through vomit later on. I loved Lucky Charms, but I didn't think that the pot of gold mixed with vomit would work. I settled on grabbing a can of diet Coke and a piece of dry toast.

I nibbled on my toast, trying desperately to reflect on what had transpired the night before. Besides my raging affair with Jack and having a ménage with several pizza boxes, I remembered Miles paying me a visit. I also recalled a shower, my poof, and he slipping me into bed, mumbling something about promising to tell me something. I heard my phone buzz, and hoped that it was him. But it was a text from Ryan.

Ryan: Jimmy's pizza called me last night. They said you put me down as an emergency contact in case you ordered more than three pizzas.

Moxie: I had a bit of a rough night.

Ryan: Ordering five pizzas and a side of bread sticks with extra oil qualifies as more than a rough night.

Moxie: Is this an intervention?

Ryan: I think we passed intervention and established a direct connection with the Betty Ford Clinic.

Moxie: Fuck off.

Ryan: Tom and I already did this morning, thank you. Want to meet for coffee after school?

Moxie: Fine, Douche Canoe.
Ryan: Wow, things must be bad. Your insults are pathetic. See
*   you then. SMOOCH*

I didn't know if I wanted to rehash the whole incident with Ryan, about David and what happened. The last thing I wanted to do was discuss how my body apparently had more rolls than Benny's Bakery. It wasn't like I didn't realize my size. However, my stepmother dreamed of having a stick-thin daughter so we can shop at Bebe's and Forever 21.

I grabbed my bag for work and walked down the stairs, since the elevator was broken. I'd forgotten to check my mail the whole weekend, so I stopped by the mailboxes and opened the little box with my name on it. I sifted through the bills and junk mail, but ran across a white letter that just had my name on the front. There was no return address. I was beginning to wonder if I should handle it with gloves in case it was a ransom note. But I didn't have anything worth being held for ransom.

Moxie,
*   I want to have dinner with you next weekend. I will make sure that Dillion is taken care of so there will be no distractions. There are some things that I want to explain to you.*

Miles

The mystery continued. I would have to get Scooby and the gang together. I was starting to convince myself that Miles was really a secret agent, maybe something like Tom Cruise in Mission Impossible. And what did it mean that he was making sure Dillion was "taken care of"? Panic started to rumble deep in my stomach. Was he planning to "off" his kid in order to run away with his brunette? From my knowledge of the mob, when you "take care" of someone, you make sure their bodies are never found. Well, at least that was what I'd learned on the Sopranos.

The letter bothered me all the way until I got to school. I dropped my things off in my classroom and headed to the teachers' lounge. I was about to pour myself a cup of liquid shit when Amber walked in. Yes, it was official, God did have it out for me.

"Well, Moxie, nice of you to dress up as Free Willy this morning." She looked at me like a snake waiting to strike its prey.

"Amber. I'm glad you were finally able to get your head out of your ass. I bet it smelled bad in there. Although, since you think your shit smells like roses, I suppose it wasn't so bad," I retaliated.

"I had a chance to talk to Dillion's dad at the school camp-out. He seriously has one tight ass. I bet you can bounce coins off that thing."

She was trying to hit me at the core and rile me up. Amber had probably seen me talking to him and wanted to stick her claws in him. I tried to play it cool. I looked at her nonchalantly as I replied, "I suppose, with your porn film history, he wanted to know if you spit or swallow."

I hit my mark. Her face turned beet red and she curled her lips into a sneer. "Do you think of anything besides sex?"

I mixed my shit coffee with the spoon and said, "Sure I do. I have a daily diary of my bowel movements and rate them by color, size and fragrance."

"You are a horrible human being." She pushed past me, storming through the door.

I shouted behind her, "You should have seen today's shit. Jagged, green and smelled like sewer. I named it after you."

At that exact moment Renee came wheezing through the door. "Amber causing trouble again?" she asked with sympathy.

"Oh, no, we were just exchanging morning pleasantries. You know, like, how was your weekend? What did you do? Isn't Sea World missing their whale?"

Renee just shook her head, but then crossed her arms over her chest. "Where the fuck have you been? I called you and sent you a million texts."

"I moved to Amsterdam for the weekend and was working in the Red Light district. They're very strict on cell phone usage." I sipped my shit coffee and leaned against the counter.

"Well, I hope that all worked out for you. Now tell me what the hell really happened."

She still had her arms crossed and was looking at me like a parent scolding their child.

"My date with David was a clusterfuck and Miles came to my place when I was drunk and gave me a shower."

Renee stood there with her mouth hanging open. "There are so many parts of that sentence that we need to obsess over, I don't know where to start."

"I'm meeting Ryan for coffee after school. Why don't you join us for a lively discussion on how Moxie can self-detonate?" I pouted.

"Dramatic much?" She switched her hands to her hips to continue her scolding.

"It involves Martha and weight management." I stared back.

Renee stood up straight and the expression on her face changed to sympathy. She knew how Martha was constantly on me about my weight. "I'll buy the cookies and extra espresso."

I nodded my head and we both left the teachers' lounge to get to our classes. The kids came shuffling in like endangered servants ready to do my bidding. I saw Dillion and felt a sense of relief, knowing that someone hadn't "taken care" of him. He came up to me, looking not quite himself.

"Hi, Miss Summers," he said so quietly that I could barely hear him. I bent down so we could talk eye to eye.

"Everything ok, Dillion?" I rubbed his arm up and down in a sympathetic gesture.

"Yeah, I haven't been sleeping great. Dad gave me this note to give to you."

I took the piece of paper from him, but my mind immediately went to Miles humping his brunette so loud that they kept Dillion up all night. The bitch obviously had no sympathy for a young child's growth development. Although, if I were with Miles, I didn't think that I'd be doing a whole lot of sleeping either. I opened the note and quickly read the contents.

Meet me at Dip It at 7:00 Saturday. – Miles

Dip It was a fondue restaurant, with small intimate booths and romantic atmosphere. I was almost banned from there because I refused to let my pot of cheese go without scraping the bottom.

"Go ahead and put your book bag away and go to the carpet for morning meeting."

My concern still loomed when Katie approached me.

"What are you selling today, Katie?" I tried to keep my sarcasm to a minimum.

She looked at me with what I could only describe as disgust. "I'm not selling anything, Miss Summers, but I want to talk about what we're learning in science."

"You mean about the weather?" I replied dryly.

"Yeah, you said when it gets so cold in winter, that you can stick your tongue on a pole and it will get stuck. I think that's a stupid lie," she said with a huff.

"Katie, do you remember what I said about hypotheses?"

"You mean ideas you can test?" she questioned.

"That's diffidently an idea you should test."

After school, Renee and I met Ryan at the coffee shop. My favorite barista wasn't working, so I had to work my magic with the new guy to get a couple of extra shots of espresso. I hoped he didn't actually believe I would blow him in the back of the store.

We all sat at the table in the back of the café. Luckily, it was crowded, so no one else would be able to listen to the horror story that was my dating life. I took a nice long sip of my coffee and broke apart the chocolate donut I got as comfort food.

Ryan, looking devastating handsome, patted his knees and cooed. "Come here and tell your Uncle Ryan what happened."

I glowered at him. "Unless Uncle Ryan feels like being castrated and using his own dick to fuck himself, I would advise cutting out the baby shit."

"That bad," he said.

I emptied my mouth, swallowing. "No, bad is when you eat White Castle at three a.m. and wake up in the morning with explosive diarrhea. What happened takes on a whole new meaning."

Renee gave me a sympathetic glance. "Did he have a small penis? That's always devastating when that happens."

"No. Apparently David was using me for my body."

"You say that like it's a bad thing," Ryan said as he sipped his green tea.

"To make a disastrous story short, Martha conned him into dating me so I would drop some weight and try out for Miss Skinny Bitch Universe. He works with a sporting equipment company and they are trying to launch a new diet plan. He wanted me to be the guinea pig. Then Miles came over when I was piss-ass drunk, took a shower with me and put me naked in my bed."

"Wow. Does Miles have a nice body?" Ryan asked with excitement.

"Focus," I said to him.

"Honey, I'm sorry that happened. Not about the Miles and the shower part, but David obviously has no penis and that's why he can't appreciate all of your awesomeness," Ryan said as he threw his arm around me in a half-way hug.

"So what are you going to do about Miles?" Renee asked.

"That's the other thing. He wants me to meet him Saturday at Dip It so we can talk."

"Weren't you banned from there?" Ryan asked with a smirk.

"It is not my fault that the chocolate fondue ended up down my shirt. I was trying to lick it clean and for some reason that seems to be too obscene for some people."

"Maybe this time Miles can lick it off your chest," Ryan said with a wink.

"Listen, perv, I'll let Miles lick chocolate off me if you let Tom lick it off your asshole."

"That's already happened," he smiled proudly.

"That's vile!" Renee exclaimed.

"Hey, don't knock it until you've tried it," Ryan said.

"But with Raj, he'll probably want you to be slathered in curry," I teased.

"Moxie, that is such a stereotype. Just because Raj is Indian doesn't mean he likes curry."

Ryan and I eyed each other, worried that we'd just pissed off Renee. But then she broke out in a smile.

"Ok," she said, blushing. "We already did that."

The three of us burst out with laughter. At that moment, I was grateful to have my best friends help me calm the nerves that were raging through my body.

Chapter Fourteen

At about three o'clock I was really beginning to panic. I had pulled at least a dozen outfits from my closet, ranging from modest teacher to fuck-me-on-the-table. Nothing seemed to work. I also questioned whether I should wear a cute matching bra and panty set or not. Wait, what was I thinking? I wasn't going to let this man suck me into his Miles-like trance and get me on my back. He had a woman at home and I was his son's teacher. But I couldn't help but imagine Miles and how his eyes pierced right through my heart when he looked at me. Bastard.

I pulled out my phone to text Ryan for some last-minute advice.

Moxie: I have no clothes to wear and decided that I have a better chance going naked anyway.
Ryan: Well, that's one way to scare him off.
Moxie: Dickhead.

Ryan: Hmm, I can tell that you're genuinely nervous if the only comeback you have is Dickhead.

Moxie: I have no idea what to expect.

Ryan: Sex. Lots of it.

Moxie: You know it's not that simple.

Ryan: You're right. Sex and a swag bag to thank him.

Moxie: SERIOUS.

Ryan: Ok, calm down. It will be fine. Just go in there with the sexy Moxie look and give him that Moxie attitude.

Moxie: But I want him to talk to me again after tonight.

Ryan: Good point. Go in black and don't speak.

I decided to be classy, yet sexy. I went with a black A-line dress and fire engine red heels. I am not the type of girl to obsess over shoes, but with 4 inches and a peep toe point, even I had to admit, they were hot. I left my hair down and added simple jewelry to complete the outfit.

I was standing in front of Dip It, feeling like a girl ready to go down on a guy for the first time. My first time giving a blow job had been when I was 16, with Jordan Swartzman. We belonged to the same temple and we were in confirmation class together. He was a cute kid with brown shaggy hair that hid his brown eyes. He was on the track team at another high school, which meant he was tall and lean, which, for being a Jewish boy, was a Hanukah miracle. He had gotten a new car for his 16th birthday and, to celebrate this, he'd asked me to go with him to the local forest reserve.

When we got there, he asked if I'd ever blown a guy before. I didn't want to seem like a complete prude, and said that I had with fake enthusiasm. The last thing I wanted was him spreading a rumor around that I was anti-penis. We sat, parked, in a secluded spot of the reserve. Jordan undid his belt and pulled his jeans and boxers to his knees. I sat there frozen, because I'd never been face to face, or face to crotch, with the one-eyed snake. I proceeded to put his dick in my mouth and bobbed my head up and down like I had seen in videos. Right as Jordan was going to spread his seed down my throat, a police officer tapped the window. We got a stern lecture from the cop, with a side discussion of safe sex. Every time since then, I had to look around before I agreed to suck on the pickle.

Coming out of the memory, I put my big girl panties on and opened the door of the restaurant. I loved the atmosphere of Dip It. It was warm and romantic, with booths, so you could lick your cheese in semi-privacy. I looked around the warm rich walls and the lush cushions of the waiting area, but I did not see Miles.

The knot in my stomach tightened. If Miles was going to play his M.O. and ditch me at the restaurant, I was going to seriously take the fondue fork to stab someone's eye out. That's after I ate all their cheese fondue. There is no need to waste perfection.

"Moxie."

I turned around to see Miles walking through the door. The knot that was previously squeezing my stomach now reached my throat. Miles stood there in charcoal dress pants and a deep blue dress shirt that was rolled up to his fabulous biceps. To top it off, he sported my favorite five o'clock shadow.

"Sorry I'm running a little behind, I had some trouble getting out the door."

Your brunette giving you shit about where you were going?

He took a few strides to get to me. He stood so close, I could smell his cologne wafting through the air. It was intoxicating, a mix of musk and Miles. I closed my eyes and took a deep breath to inhale his scent. I imagined us laying in bed together, my nose snuggled between his neck and his jaw, sucking in his sweet scent. I just wanted to lick my way across his neck and down his chest…

"You ok?"

I snapped my eyes open, realizing that I had my tongue sticking slightly out of my mouth.

"Yeah, of course. I was just inhaling the…cheese. I could almost feel it on my tongue," I lied.

"Well, we certainly don't want you to have to wait. You might dive into someone else's booth and I'll have to indulge on my own," he said as he put his hand on my lower back to follow the hostess.

Our hostess led us to the back of the restaurant, where there was a small intimate booth. It looked like it was made for only one person and I was interested to see how someone with healthy hips and a tall hunk of meat were going to fit. I slid in first and Miles scooted next to me, living little room between us.

"You look beautiful," he said as he handed me my menu.

"Thanks. You look very G.Q." I smiled shyly.

"I especially like the shoes," he pointed under the table. "They leave a lot to the imagination."

"They're shoes, there's not much to imagine." I leaned in to whisper into his ear. "They have feet inside."

He turned his head so our lips almost touched. His eyes turned down to my lips. "I was imagining them swung over my shoulders while I have my head…"

"Hello my name is Sam. I'll be your waiter. What can I get you to drink?"

Miles rotated to face the waiter. "I'll just stick with water right now, thanks. Moxie?"

I hadn't moved. I was too stunned at what he was starting to say. I blinked a few times and looked at the waiter. "I'll take a dirty martini. Extra dirty."

The waiter eyed me. "Haven't you been here before?"

"Nope! Never," I quickly replied.

The waiter looked at me for a few extra seconds, then walked away.

Miles turned back to face me. "Nervous?" he asked.

He'd seen me twisting the napkin in my hands. I threw it in my lap and rightened myself so I wouldn't give my emotions away. "No. Is there any reason to be?"

Of course I was nervous. First, I thought his brunette might find out that he was out with me, and second, I was afraid that the waiter was going to recognize me as the cheesy boob girl.

Miles took my hand in his and ran his thumb over my knuckles. I had forgotten how that felt. The last time I could soberly remember was in the tent during the school camp-out.

The night he gave me an orgasm to ruin all orgasms. The night he ditched me…again. That thought had me pulling my hands back to myself, and I could see his smile fall.

"Thanks for meeting me tonight," he said. "There's a lot that I need to tell you."

Could it be that you are with someone else? That you've enjoyed having me be a plaything and now you want to make it up to me by stuffing me with glorious cheese?

"Why do you keep disappearing?"

It seems as though I wasn't even going to let the steam start on the fondue pot before I started my interrogation.

"Disappearing?" he asked.

"Yeah. Like all the times you either get me completely worked up and disappear, or you give me an orgasm that breaks me in half and then you're out of sight. I know you have someone waiting at home. So why are you playing this game with me? I've been played enough recently."

It was then I realized that meeting Miles here had been a bad idea. I was not a stupid girl, and the fact that I was letting men trample over me was starting to piss me off. To top it off, what the hell was I doing with a guy who was cheating on his girlfriend and was a parent of one of my students?

"You're right, I do have someone waiting for me at home."

My heart sank. Even though I mentally knew he had someone else, I was still hoping he felt the same attraction.

"Then why did you have me meet you for dinner? Why would you do all those things to me?"

Miles's face turned to confusion. "I said I do have someone waiting for me at home. Dillion."

"I know you have Dillion. What about your other woman?"

"What other woman?" he said.

Oh, this was cliché, the whole I'm-going-to-pretend-there-isn't-anyone-else-because-I'm-really-a-schizophrenic-asshole.

"The brunette. The one at the park. I know you live with her and she calls you when we're together. Is that when the bells go off in your head, remembering that you've got someone else who is probably waiting for you to come home and fuck her senseless? I know that if you were mine, I wouldn't let you out of the fucking bed. I'd tie your ass up, and keep you there, afraid that there are other ho-bags like me trying to…"

"Whoa…Moxie, stop." He threw his hands up to his chest, motioning me to calm down. "If I ever hear you call yourself anything but beautiful, intelligent and funny, I'll have to tie YOU up and spank the stupid out of you."

That had me shut up.

"Let's address all of these things one by one. There is no other woman. Well, that's not completely true. That brunette you were talking about is my sister."

I sat in silence, wondering if I should give him shit for trying to pull the sister card on me, but then he continued.

"I was planning on moving from Maine, but the freelance art position came up faster then I was expecting, so we had to come sooner than planned. I had no time to find a place for Dillion and I, so she offered to have us stay with her."

I thought back to my earlier discussion with Dillion about where they were staying, and he did say something about being with his Aunt. I felt bile rise in my throat. I had automatically jumped to the conclusion that she was Miles's girlfriend. I was definitely getting the award for biggest asshat of the year.

"My disappearing is why I wanted to talk to you tonight. Well, that and other reasons." His left eyebrow popped up and a devilish smile swept across his face. I went back to playing with the napkin in my hands. "The reason I keep skipping out is because of Dillion."

"Dillion?" I asked, confused.

"Dillion is suffering from PTSD."

"Post traumatic stress disorder?"

"When we were in Maine, my wife and Dillion were in a severe car accident. My wife did not survive, but Dillion did, and had several severe injuries. He was in a medically induced coma for a few days. They had to reset some bones in his arm and leg."

"Miles, I am so sorry," I said softly. My heart ached not only for Miles's loss, but thinking of sweet Dillion laying helplessly in the hospital, in pain, made my stomach twist.

"Thankfully, he healed physically." He paused and took in a deep breath. "But mentally, he has really suffered."

"I can't even begin to imagine," I said. "But he seems to do well in class. The only thing that has ever stuck out is that he keeps to himself a lot, but I attributed that to the fact that he is insanely smart and the rest of my class are big dumb asses."

At that, Miles laughed. "He's always been a smart kid. The trouble is more at night. He gets bad night terrors. It tears me apart when I hear him screaming and crying. I run into his room, but he's not even fully awake. It's like he's reliving the accident all over again. He's started working with a child psychologist. She's really great with him and gives me ideas for things to do when he has anxiety attacks. The calls I get are from my sister when he's having a bad anxiety episode. She doesn't know how to handle it like I do."

"I have to be honest. I don't even know what to say," I said in an awkward whisper.

"I don't want you to say anything about it. I wanted you to know. You're his teacher and he respects you."

"You could have waited until conferences."

"True, but I needed to explain why I kept leaving you. It wasn't you, Moxie, ever. You are beyond sexy, even though that mouth of yours needs to be taught a lesson."

"But I'm the one who's a teacher," I said with a sly smile.

Miles moved closer to me, leaning in to the side of my head to whisper in my ear. "Then maybe you can teach me how to make you scream my name."

I felt my whole body flush with warm heat. He certainly didn't beat around the bush. I was seriously hoping that he wouldn't beat around my bush either.

"Let's eat so we can have dessert," he continued.

"They have the best milk chocolate fondue," I said, trying to ignore the ache between my thighs."

"I'm sure they do," he said. "But I can say with almost certainty that the chocolate would be much better if I could lick it off your stomach."

Chapter Fifteen

Dinner was amazing. I'm not sure if I enjoyed Miles or the cheese more. We talked about everything and anything. Miles told me about how he got into the art world, and that he liked to paint and sculpt as well as do graphic design work. He even told me about his wife and what life was like living in Maine. I wasn't at all insecure when he spoke of his wife. I knew that she was a part of him and Dillion. But it was also in the past. I enjoyed hearing about what a great mom she was and how Dillion had so many of her attributes. I was happy for Dillion and could only hope that he would be able to hold on to the positive memories of his mom.

I was also worried about him and what Miles had shared with me. Dillion was a special kid, and not only because I wanted Miles, but because he was smart, funny and wise beyond his years. For a brief minute I thought about what he would think if Miles and I dated. Would that be weird? Would he feel like I was trying to take over his mom's memory? I didn't bring this up with Miles. Mainly because I didn't know where this attraction I had towards Miles was going.

"You're not really going to scrape the bowl with the pound cake, are you?" Miles said with a laugh.

"The hell I'm not. That chocolate is too damn good to waste. It would be a crime against humanity."

"That's one of the things I really like about you, Moxie. You're not afraid to eat."

I paused with the fondue fork in my hand. The insecure feeling that David had placed in my head started to make its way forward. I put the fork on the plate.

"What's wrong?" Miles looked at me with concern.

"Umm, I probably ate too much," I said, feeling my face turn red.

Miles grabbed my fondue fork and scraped the last bit of chocolate onto the poundcake. Then he brought the fork over to my lips. I took the bite into my mouth without looking away from his eyes, which now were dark.

"I don't ever want you to feel self-conscious with me. I love the way your body is." He pressed a kiss on my cheek. "And I love watching your mouth when you bite into your food." He pressed another kiss on my other cheek. "And I fantasize what it would be like if your mouth was wrapped around my cock instead." He kissed my lips, sucking off any of the chocolate that was still left on them.

I let out a disapproving groan when his mouth left mine. I wanted those lips all over me.

"Come home with me?" When it came out, it sounded more like a beg.

"What about Dillion and your sister?" I asked. "Won't it be awkward if you come home with a woman?"

"Dillion will be asleep. My sister knows I'm out with you and she also knows I'm a man who is starting to date again."

"So this is a date?" I asked with amusement.

"If it isn't, I just paid a shitload for a parent/teacher conference," he laughed. "I would say let's go to your place, but I need to be home in case Dillion needs me."

"I understand."

"We'll leave your car here and I'll bring you back in the morning."

"A sleepover? That's being a little presumptuous, Mr. Dane."

"Miss Summers, what I plan to do to you tonight will have you so worn out that driving would be hazardous to mankind."

With that, I grabbed my purse and Miles helped me out of the booth. When I stood up Miles gave my ass a little pinch and I yelped. I glanced over my shoulder to him and he looked at me like a boy who'd just put a frog down a girl's dress.

Miles opened the passenger door of his Jeep Cherokee for me. I was about to get in when he stopped me and turned me so my back was against the car. His mouth slammed onto mine, opening so our tongues could find each other to embrace. I dropped my purse onto the ground . My hands flew up to his head and I tangled my fingers in his hair. He put his hands on my waist, squeezing until it almost hurt. He kissed me like he wanted to swallow me, deep and wanting. When he pressed against me, I could feel his erection trying to break free of his pants.

He pulled away and pressed his forehead to mine. "Sorry, I couldn't help myself. I've been sitting in that damn restaurant with a hard-on, waiting to taste you."

"I probably taste like chocolate-covered cheese." I laughed.

"Yeah, you kind of do. But I have a way to fix that."

"You have a mint in your car?"

"No. I have something sweet and salty you can suck on," he said with a devious smile.

"If you play your cards right, I might suck, then swallow," I teased.

He let out a loud groan. "Get in the car, woman, or I'm going to come in my pants, like a teenager."

I thought about a teenage Miles while I got into the car. I bet he'd been sexy even as a teen. Miles got in the driver's seat and turned on the engine. I peeked at him from the corner of my eye. He looked delicious and I wanted to devour him. That was when I decided I was going to play dirty. I twisted in my seat and moved my hand from my knee. I felt him tense and grip the wheel harder. I slowly moved my hand up his leg to his thigh, and then to the hard bulge in his pants. I reached over and started kissing his neck, sucking some skin before I let go.

"Moxie, are you trying to get us in an accident?" he said, trying hard to concentrate on the road.

"You said I could have something sweet to suck on. Your neck seemed like a good option. I'll find the salty later," I whispered.

"Fucking Christ," he said.

"I'm a Jew, Miles. We don't believe in Christ." I chuckled in his ear.

To my disappointment, the ride was short. I liked teasing Miles, but I also knew there would be more when we got inside.

We pulled into the driveway and Miles came around to open my car door. "Such a gentleman," I said.

"In five minutes, I promise you, there will be nothing gentle about this man."

He kissed me swiftly and took my hand as we headed to the front door. Miles's sister's house was moderately sized, with brown siding and red brick. We got to the front door and he paused before opening it. He turned me to him and looked deep into my eyes. This gave me the opportunity to truly see the color of his eyes, which I knew were blue, but also contained some specks of green. His expression turned serious.

"I don't bring random girls home to fuck them. It wouldn't be fair to Dillion to have women parading through here, and it's not the type of man I am. In fact, I haven't felt like this since my wife passed."

The mention of his deceased wife gave me a small pang in my stomach. I might have been flippant about sex in the past, but that wasn't what I was feeling with Miles. I also didn't want to compete with a dead woman. "Miles, maybe this isn't a good idea."

"What? Fuck. I didn't mean that you are just a fling I want to screw to try to get over my grief. I've dealt with the loss and yes, she will always be a part of my past. I want to move on. I want to move on with you."

My heart felt like it could leap across the world. "I want this too," I confessed.

He slammed his mouth back onto mine, seeking my tongue to intertwine with his. I reached my hands back up into his hair and pulled at it slightly. I heard him let out a groan deep in the back of his throat. He pulled back and searched for the right key to let us into the house. When the door unlocked, he held it open and gestured for me to go in. He followed behind, pinching my ass. I now understood that he liked to be behind me so he could have access to my rear and pinch it at his leisure.

When we went into the living room, I saw the brunette sitting on the couch next to a bald-headed guy. The brunette turned to see us. "Hey, you're back," she said to Miles. "You must be Moxie." She stood up from the couch and extended her hand. "I'm Kelly, Miles's sister."

"Nice to meet you," I said, feeling the relief that this woman was actually in no way sexually connected to Miles.

"This is John, my boyfriend."

He stood up to shake my hand as well. He was tall, but not as tall as Miles. He had a red goatee and a slim frame. "Dillion is sleeping, and we were just about to turn in as well." Kelly moved to Miles and I could hear her tell him that Dillion was sleeping soundly and hadn't woken up from nightmares.

"Thanks, guys, for watching him tonight," Miles said.

"You know it's such a hard chore, watching my amazing nephew," Kelly teased. "Moxie, it was a pleasure finally meeting you. I've heard so much about you from Dillion and, of course, Miles." She winked at Miles like she'd just revealed a secret as she took John's hand and headed toward the stairs.

As soon as they disappeared, Miles spun me around to face him.

"Hi," he said softly.

"Hi," I replied, looking up at him, smiling.

"Would you like a tour?"

"Is it of your body? Because the answer would be, fuck, yes."

"What are we going to do with that dirty mouth?"

"I have a few ideas that might be intriguing." I licked my tongue across my lower lip. He bent to kiss me and retraced the area I'd just licked with my own tongue. My insides twisted with anticipation and my Maidenhead was set to sail.

Miles took my face in his hands and kissed me with heated passion. He darted out his tongue, pressing my lips to open. He wasn't asking for an invitation, he was demanding I gave in. His hands moved to take the light coat I was wearing off my shoulders; it pooled onto the floor. I traced my hands over his shirt and felt his glorious muscles underneath.

To say the man was ripped would be an understatement. He carried a six pack that I wanted to open and drink in. I had to pause a moment, to take it all in. There was a little part of me that wondered, why me? The girl whose mother would go out of her way to try to find ways to drop her weight. I started to feel self-conscious of my body.

Miles sensed something was bothering me. "What's wrong?"

"Why me?" I looked up at him.

"Why you what?"

"Why do you want me when you can have some skinny bitch who eats salads only and then pukes them up because she felt she ate too much?"

He laughed. "Because, Moxie…" He stopped and pressed a feather-light kiss on my mouth. "It isn't about weight…" Another kiss. "Or how much you eat or don't eat…" Another kiss. "You have a presence about you that draws me in. Your wit, your brain, and I love your curves. If you don't believe my words, let my body tell you."

He reached down and put his arms under my knees to lift me into his arms.

"What are you doing? You're going to hurt yourself!"

"Moxie, you have two point five seconds to shut up or I'm going to spank your ass so hard that it could be used as a stop sign."

Even though the thought excited me, I decided to shut my trap. He carried me up the stairs and into the third bedroom on the left. I assumed this was the one he took up residence in. He put me down, softy, letting me get my bearings after he'd manhandled me.

"I thought about you being in this room a lot," he said as he pressed his palm against my face.

"Really? And what exactly did you think about?" I teased.

He smiled, knowing that I was urging him to tell me his fantasies.

"You, spread out naked on my bed."

"That's a typical fantasy."

"I wasn't finished. You are spread out, hands bound to the headboard. Your legs are spread wide and my face is buried between your thighs, sucking, licking, making you scream my name."

"That's a little more vivid," I said as my breath started to speed up.

His mouth returned to mine and he pressed himself close to me, his arousal apparent, rubbing against my stomach. His hands slipped underneath the hem of my dress to find a very bare ass.

"You're not wearing panties?" he asked with surprise.

"It's laundry day. I had nothing clean to wear," I teased and winked to let him know that I was joking.

"Never do laundry again," he breathed into my neck.

His hands reached around to find my very wet and very needy Pound Puppy.

"Fuck! You're so damn wet," he cried.

I decided that Miles was wearing way too many clothes at this point. I frantically ripped at his shirt, popping buttons along the way. Then I got to see his glorious naked chest. With a sprinkling of hair along his pecs and a trail leading to the pot of gold.

Our kissing continued as I fumbled to get his belt undone. He realized that I was having a problem multi-tasking and he performed the simple task himself. Once let free, I pulled down his pants, along with his boxer briefs. I stilled, looking at the impressive length that stood before me. His erection was perfect. Not like cute-puppy perfect. Like I-hope-to-God-it-fits perfect.

"Moxie, you're going to give me a complex, looking at me like that."

"Sorry, I can't help it. I was trying to figure out the logistics of moving my organs around so that would fit inside me."

He gathered my dress, starting at the hem, and pulled it up over my body. I'd decided on my pink bra with lace trim, something to suggest sexy, but also fun and flirty.

"Holy shit, I want to get lost in those tits," he moaned, grabbing my breasts.

He reached around to unhook my bra and bent down to take my tight nipple into his mouth. I released a moan, squeezing my eyes shut at the feeling of pure pleasure.

"How do you like to be taken? Do you want me to bend you over the bed? Or spread your legs wide and put them up on my shoulders?"

The ache between my legs was consuming me. I'd had my fair share of lovers, but no one talked dirty to me the way Miles was talking. The foreplay was intoxicating, and I could just explode by his words alone.

"I don't care how you take me, but if you don't take me now I might explode," I managed to huff out.

Miles guided me to the bed. I climbed on it, moving to the middle. Miles crawled above my body until his form was blanketed over me. His eyes stared deep into mine as if he was trying to communicate something telepathically.

"You're beautiful," he whispered.

"Thank you," I replied. "You're not exactly the Hunchback of Notre Dame."

Miles propped himself up on his hands and started trailing kisses down my neck onto my chest. He took my left breast into his mouth and sucked my nipple until there was pain. It felt delicious and I didn't want him to stop, but he continued his journey down to my stomach and stopped right before hitting the apex of my thighs. He looked up at me, hands resting on each thigh, spreading me open.

"I'm going to taste you, make you come hard, and then bury myself deep inside you."

My breath hitched at his words and then I felt his warm, supple tongue hit directly were I craved it. He swirled his tongue around my clit and I threw my hands in his hair. I pushed my hips up, trying to gain more friction, to relieve the build-up he was creating. I felt him stick his fingers inside me, in and out, twisting and turning.

I felt my climax low in my stomach, escalating fast. My heart was beating so fast that it almost stole my breath away with each pulse. His tongue swirled faster and the speed of his fingers increased. He pulled away for a brief moment.

"Damn it Moxie, come for me now," he said through gritted teeth.

That was all that it took to send me into bliss. My orgasm shook through me, curling my toes. I felt myself holding my breath, not wanting the feeling to end. I faintly heard the drawer on the nightstand open, and the rip of a condom wrapper. Then Miles moved upwards and plunged himself inside me while I was still riding the waves of my release. He moved his hips, fast, as he buried his face into my neck.

"So tight, so beautiful, so perfect," he grunted.

"Miles, I'm going to come again."

"Together," was all he could manage to say as he bucked his hips, sinking into me quickly.

As I started to feel the second wave, Miles moved his hips into me one, two, three more times.

"Fuuuuck, Moxie," he growled as he found his release. My second orgasm followed, matching the first in intensity.

Sweat covered both of us. Miles rolled off me and lay on the bed. I could hear that he was still breathing hard. He turned his head to me. "That was…"

"Fucktastic," I concluded.

He took my hand, brought it to his lips and brushed my knuckles with soft kisses. He moved and pulled the sheets, which were now in disarray over the bed, up to cover us both. He turned onto his side and patted the bed, signaling for me to spoon with him.

I followed his directions, choosing not to argue about who would be big spoon and who, the little spoon. My body curled into his and his arm draped around my waist. He buried his face into my hair and took a deep breath. That was the last thing I remembered as I drifted into sleep.

Chapter Sixteen

Screaming. My eyes flew open and I felt disoriented until I remembered I was in Miles's bed. More screaming, coming from outside the room. I turned to wake up Miles, but saw that he was already gone. The screaming was coming from a child, from Dillion. I found the clock and it said two forty-one. I remembered what Miles told me about Dillion getting night terrors, but I wasn't sure what to do. So I followed my instinct.

I found Miles's shirt on the floor and threw it over my naked frame. I stepped out of the door, following the cries until I found Dillion's room. I peered inside to see Miles cradling Dillion in his arms, rocking him back and forth, reassuring him that he was safe.

"It's ok, buddy, you're safe," Miles cooed into Dillion's ear.

My heart wanted to bleed. A boy so young that had been through so much.

I walked into the room, suddenly scared that Miles was going to yell at me to leave. He saw me and his eyes were full of worry. I wasn't sure if it was because I was witnessing Dillion's pain, or if his son would ever be able to heal completely.

"What can I do?" I whispered to Miles, but he didn't answer me.

I bent down next to Dillion's bed, rubbing his leg as Miles rocked him.

"Dillion, sweetie, it's Miss Summers. You're ok and safe in your bed," I soothed.

At that point I didn't care if Dillion knew I was there as his dad's lover. I just wanted his pain to end.

Miles and I continued to soothe Dillion until the crying stopped and he fell back into a regular sleep. Miles lowered him back onto the bed and we both stood up. Miles kissed Dillion's forehead and turned to me. I wasn't even sure if Dillion had actually woken up, but I saw his steady breathing and knew the night terror had ended.

Miles took my hand and held it tight within his own as he lead me back to his room.

When we got there, I didn't know what to say. I wasn't sure if it was something we should have talked about. But Miles was silent as he unbuttoned his shirt that I was wearing until my bare skin hit the cool air. He kissed me, but it wasn't urgent, like it had been before. This time it was soft and slow as he moved his hands up and down my naked back.

He took me into his bed, still kissing me. We both lay on our sides, facing each other. I draped one of my legs over his hip and he moved closer to me. He looked into my eyes and stroked his left hand over my hip to caress my lower back.

I rocked towards him, knowing want he wanted. It wasn't about the sex, it was about the intimacy. What Dillion had gone through scared him, and he needed to know that someone was there to comfort him as well. I wanted to be that someone for him.

"I need you," he whispered.

"You have me," I said as I traced the outside of his lips.

I decided to take the plunge. "Do you want to talk about it?"

He squeezed my hip. "It just shakes me up when I hear him scream like that. I would do anything to take it away from him."

"I know." I wiped a strand of hair that fell onto his forehead. "But you're an amazing dad and you are doing everything for him. I wish there was more I could do."

"The only thing you have to do right now is be here with me."

"I think I can do that." I smiled. "Plus, my car is still at the restaurant and I'm too lazy to walk." I winked.

"What would have happened if I didn't partake in your survey at the bar that night?" he asked with his lips curled up in a smile.

I chuckled softly. "You mean, what if you ignored the loud sloppy drunk accusing you of having hairy balls?"

"Well, I could have done without the loud sloppy drunk, but I was drawn to your spunk and your honesty. And then, when I found out that you were Dillion's teacher, I knew something was meant to happen."

"How romantically sweet of you," I teased.

I felt a small whack on my ass cheek.

"Ow!" I cried, trying to keep my voice down.

"That's what you get when you tease," he said, but he couldn't hide his own amusement.

"Come on, you knew there was something there, too," he said.

"I did. But I thought, for sure the vomit on your shoes would have been a turn off."

"Which time?" he said with a smirk.

This time I reached around and slapped his ass cheek. He brought his hand under my ribs and started to tickle me playfully. I thrashed around, trying to escape his grip, while also trying not to howl in laughter. I moved to straddle him, trying to get the upper-hand in out tickle war. The sheet from the bed slid down off the top of my body and pooled at my waist.

Miles stopped tickling me and his expression became intense. I could feel his erection growing and pressing under me. His hand went from my waist and grazed up from my stomach to cup each breast. My back arched, pushing my breasts further into his palms. At first he slowly kneaded them, and then took each nipple between his fingers, rolling the swollen buds.

"Agh!" I exclaimed, throwing my head back in pleasure. I moved my arms to his chest and raked my nails over his chest, grabbing the hair that covered it.

Miles let out a hiss between his teeth, indicating that the bite of pain from my clawing was welcome. I ground my hips against him, circling around his now very thick erection. I moved my body down his waist, pulling the sheet away with me. His naked body was exposed and I took a minute to enjoy the view.

"See something you like?" he quipped.

"Not particularly, but I suppose I'll have to make do," I answered sarcastically.

"I see I'm going to have to teach that snarky mouth of yours a lesson."

"Not if my snarky mouth is going to be occupied."

"And how is that?" he asked.

I lowered my head and kissed each of his knees, slowing kissing and nipping as I inched my way back up to the target area. When I got to the perfect plush tip of his cock, I darted my tongue out to swipe the tip. Miles let out a groan and closed his eyes.

I took the head into my mouth and swirled it with my tongue. Mentally, I was wondering if I was even going to be able to take all of Miles in my mouth without gagging. This was not the time to reprise my role of sick or drunk Moxie. I pulled Miles into my mouth slowly, until the tip of his cock hit the back of my throat.

"Oh, God, Moxie," he moaned.

I bobbed my head up and down his shaft, adding my hand to maximize the effect it was having. Miles threw his hands in my hair, clutching my scalp.

"Moxie, sweetness, you need to stop or I'm going to come in your mouth."

I drew him in and back out with a long pull and made an exaggerated popping sound when I released him. Before I could come back with a witty remark, he bent up and scooped me up by my underarms so I was once again straddling him. He leaned his torso over to the night stand to take out a condom. I grabbed the package out of his hands and ripped it open with my teeth. I took out the latex ring and rolled it down Miles's length.

"Moxie, if I don't get inside you right now I'm going to come before this even starts."

I smiled at his confession and lifted myself up enough to press his tip to the entrance of my slick heat. I took him in, painstakingly slow, until he was buried in me all the way. I let out a heavy breath before I started moving my hips in a circular motion. He grabbed my hips, indicating that it was his turn to lead the movements.

We moved in tandem, creating a rhythm that was uniquely ours. I started to pick up my pace, and both or our breaths came out harder. My heart was pounding a mile a minute, not only because of the intensity of the sex, but because of the feelings I had for this man.

"Miles, I can't hold out," I panted.

"Don't hold out, sweetness, let it go."

My orgasm ripped out of me like lightning in a storm. I wanted desperately to shout out Miles's name as it sat on the tip of my tongue, but I had to remember to stay as quiet as I could because everyone was sleeping. So, instead, I dug my nails into Miles's abdomen, riding out the waves of pleasure.

Miles sped up, catching his own release before stilling underneath me. I collapsed on top of him, sinking my face between his neck and shoulder. I could feel his pulse beating in his neck, the tempo matching my own. He kissed the top of my head and pulled himself out of me. I fell onto my back on the bed and Miles took the condom off and threw it in the trash.

He came back to bed and twisted me away from him so he could spoon me. I felt him shaking a little as he kissed my shoulder. I took his hand in mine and laid it against my stomach, telling him without words that I wasn't going anywhere.

"Thank you," he whispered.

I knew that wasn't just about the sex, but for being there for him and Dillion. I kissed the top of his head and we both feel back into sleep.

Chapter Seventeen

I opened my eyes to see a sun beam shining through the window and onto the bed sheet. I looked to my side and noticed the bed was again empty. I reflected back on the intense night that had transpired. I was unsure of how Miles was feeling after being with me or about me witnessing Dillion's night terror first hand.

I was trying to register how I was feeling about all of it when I heard the door open. I threw the sheet over myself, not knowing who was coming in the room. If it was Dillion, the last thing I wanted to do was scar him further by letting him see his naked teacher in his dad's bed.

"Are we role playing, where you are the ghost wearing a sheet and I'm the boy encroaching into its territory unwelcomed?" Miles asked.

The top of my head peeked out from under the sheet. "No, I didn't know if you were Dillion. The last thing I want to do is add to a growing therapy bill."

Miles chuckled. "He's downstairs, eating breakfast with Kelly. I came up to see if you wanted to join us."

I wasn't sure what protocol was appropriate here. Did I stay and join in the family breakfast or did I jump out of the window and do the walk of shame through the yard? It was only one story up; I didn't think I could break that many bones.

"I'm not sure that's a good idea. If you distract Dillion for a few minutes, I can sneak out without him seeing me. I don't want things to be weird because he saw his teacher at his house."

"He knows you're here," Miles said.

"What? How does he know? Are they going to call DCFS on you? Do you have a lawyer? Who is Dillion's next of kin, in case you go to jail?" I said in a panic.

"Whoa, slow down there. No one is calling DCFS, and unless you are under eighteen years old I have no plans on going to jail. Dillion knew you were here last night."

"He did?"

"He heard you in his room when he was having his nightmare."

"Oh, God," I groaned, putting my hands on my head. "I knew it was a bad idea to go in there."

Miles walked over and sat on the bed. He pulled the sheet so my entire face was now uncovered. "The first thing he asked me this morning was if he could see you. He wants to talk to you."

"Great, I'm going to be lectured by a six-year-old on what a hooch I am for sleeping with his dad and he's going to ask to be placed with another teacher."

Miles shook his head at my dramatic response. "There is a pair of sweats in the drawer if you don't want to wear your dress. Although, the thought of you in that dress with nothing underneath could have you imprisoned in my room all day."

I couldn't help but roll my eyes. "Give me a few minutes. I'll be right down."

He bent down to kiss my forehead. It was a sweet, reassuring gesture that told me last night wasn't a mistake for him and that he wasn't upset that I tried to help him with Dillion. But the real question was how did Dillion feel about me being here?

I got out of bed and opened Miles's chest of drawers to pull out some of his sweats and an oversized t-shirt. Since Miles was so tall and broad, everything I put on fit. Actually, it was baggy all around. I snuck into the hall bathroom and looked around for some toothpaste. When I found some, I squirted some on my finger and performed what I call the walk of shame brush. I ran my fingers through my just-fucked hair, so I would look somewhat presentable in front of Miles's family. I took a deep breath and headed down the stairs.

When I got there I saw Kelly and Dillion sitting at the breakfast bar. John must have been out, and Miles was standing over the stove, making pancakes. I wasn't sure if I was more turned on by his tight ass in the track pants he was wearing or the fact that he was cooking one of the foods I considered to have its own category in the food pyramid.

"There she is," Miles said, smiling. Both Kelly and Dillion looked up from their plates and I couldn't help but feel like an animal on display at the zoo.

I waved at Kelly, who smiled and waved back to me. But when I looked at Dillion, I saw dark circles encasing his eyes and his floppy brown hair tossed around like he had been on a roller coaster. I moved towards the breakfast bar, Dillion's eyes never leaving mine. I was ready for it, ready for the hefty lecture I was about to get from a six-year-old, explaining why it wasn't right for his teacher to be fucking his dad. Ok, maybe not in those exact terms.

Dillion hopped down from his seat, came around the breakfast bar and stood in front of me. I was wondering if I should put my hands forward to protect my Who Who Dilly in case he tried to bash it in. But, before I could even react, Dillion swung his arms around my waist and plastered himself to me in a hug.

"It's about time you came down. I wanted to go into my dad's room to wake you up, but he said you might not like me bouncing on your head this early," Dillion said as he released his arms from around me.

I looked at Miles, who was grinning at us as he flipped the pancakes over in the pan. I felt tears stinging the back of my eyes. This child, who had been through so much at such a young age, was welcoming me into his home. I crouched down so we were face to face.

"How are you feeling this morning?" I asked, wondering how affected he was by his nightmare.

"Ok. I don't remember most of it, but I remember you and Dad coming into the room and you patting my leg."

"Yeah, that was probably weird, for you to see your teacher in the middle of the night," I said, not wanting to address the fact that Miles and I had been going at it like rabbits only a few hours before.

"No, it was cool. I like you, Miss Summers. You're nice and funny and I like that you tell Katie where to park it."

I heard both Miles and Kelly snicker in the background at Dillion's words. For the millionth time, I wondered how old this kid really was, because there was just no way he was only six.

"Dillion, are you sure it's ok that I'm here? I mean, being your teacher is important."

"You're right, Miss Summers."

My heart sank a little, figuring that Dillion would not be ok with Miles and I being together.

"But…" he continued. "My dad likes you, so it's important that you're here, too."

He leaned in to give me another hug and then returned to his seat at the breakfast bar. Kindergarteners didn't receive letter grades on their report cards. But if they did, I would have given this kid straight A's even if he was failing every subject.

Miles came over with the pan and dropped the pancakes onto the plates. He stooped and pressed a kiss on my shoulder before going back to the stove.

"You look beautiful," he whispered in my ear.

"You're turned on by the ratty morning look, aren't you?" I teased.

He leaned in closer, so I would be the only one to hear what he said.

"No, I like the freshly fucked look."

I turned my head to look at him as he walked away and my lips curved up into a grin.

"How many pancakes would you like, Mox?"

I thought it was so cute how he called me Mox.

"Dad makes killer pancakes," Dillion chimed in. "He can even make one with the first letter of your name!"

"In that case, you can make my whole name," I said to Miles, and Dillion started clapping and bouncing up and down in his seat.

"What should we do today?" Miles asked.

I felt a little uncomfortable. I wasn't sure if that "we" included me, or if he was speaking directly to Dillion and Kelly. I didn't know what to expect, considering most of my dates ended with me sneaking out of the place and changing my phone number.

"John and I are headed to the lake, since it's going to be so nice out. You're more than welcome to join us."

"That sounds perfect. Moxie, how does that sound to you? A day at the beach," Miles said, sliding some pancakes onto my plate.

I couldn't help the relief that stirred in my chest, knowing that Miles wasn't trying to brush me off after last night.

"That sounds great," I said, sitting down and sticking a piece of pancake in my mouth. Dillion dropped his fork onto his plate and reached over his chair to wrap his arms around me.

"We can build the Willis Tower in the sand. Did you know that the Willis Tower used to be called the Sears Tower and now people in Chicago refuse to call it the Willis Tower because they say it's a crime against humanity to rename an iconic building," Dillion spouted out.

Miles, Kelly and I burst out laughing and I peeked at Miles, giving my praise to the child he so lovingly raised.

We all sat, enjoying each other's company. I must have eaten a billion of Miles's pancakes. Dillion was right, he did make killer pancakes. It was just another one of Miles's fine attributes. I heard the ping on my phone, which was in my bag, on the counter. I walked over to see that I'd received a text from David.

> *David: Moxie, I know you don't want to speak to me. But there are things that I need to explain to you. Will you please meet me so we can talk?*

Was this man insane? I couldn't believe that David even had the balls to contact me. Especially since I thought I kicked his balls in so hard, there was nothing left.

> *Moxie: Fuck off.*

David: I deserve that, but I want to talk to you. Please hear me out.

My mind flew back to the memory of David trying to convince me to become his test rabbit for his company's new diet line. I looked down at my body. Suddenly, I thought of going to the beach, and people seeing me in a bikini freaked me out. I started to feel sick to my stomach and uncomfortable. I threw my phone back into the purse and looked at Miles.

"Hey, I need to head back to my place and clean up if we're going to go out later."

I saw a look of disappointment hit Miles's face. "Sure, let me just get my keys."

"Great. I'll grab my stuff," I said as I headed up the stairs to Miles's bedroom.

I took Miles's clothes off, folded them, and went to lay them on the bed. Before I did, I held the sweatshirt up to my nose. I inhaled the scent of Miles, soothing, reassuring and masculine. I reflected back to last night, the way he touched me, made me feel like I was the only woman in the universe. I wanted his hands on me again, soon, tracing my breasts, then stroking slowly down to reach between my thighs.

I took a look around the room again, burning the memories into my head so they could hold me over until I saw him again. Downstairs, Miles was waiting for me with his car keys. Dillion was out of his seat at the breakfast bar, standing next to his dad, floppy hair a mess from his restless sleep. I bent down to talk to him.

"We probably shouldn't say anything to the other kids about me being at your house this weekend."

He looked at me, brushing his hair out of his eyes. Part of me wanted to cut it, but it made up so much of his personality. "So does this mean I get to call you Foxy?" he croaked.

"While I would be very flattered, you can call me Moxie when we're not in school."

"I know your name is Moxie, silly, but Daddy calls you Foxy, so I wanted to."

I tried not to burst out laughing when Miles interjected."Ok, ok, MOXIE has to get going," Miles said while mussing Dillion's hair, his cheeks a little flushed.

"See you a little later."

He smiled and gave me a big hug. I waved goodbye to Kelly and walked out of the door that Miles was holding open for me. We walked around to the passenger side of the car and he held it open, resting his arms on the top of the door. I went to get into the car, when he pulled the collar of my jacket towards him.

"You ok?" he asked, concern showing on his face.

"I'm great. More than great, actually. I just have stuff on my mind."

"Are you regretting last night?"

"Yes."

His face fell and he looked at me with disappointment.

"I should have taken more cheese to go," I said with a teasing smile.

"Wench," he laughed.

"I had an amazing time, Miles, the food and the dessert." I pressed a kiss on his lips.

The drive back to my car was primarily quiet. Miles asked me some questions and I replied with one-word answers. It wasn't that I was disinterested in what he was saying, but my mind was consumed with the number of cuss words I could aim at David and how he'd planted the seed of insecurity in my head.

We arrived at the restaurant and Miles pulled up next to my car. It was awkward, even though I was thrilled with what had happened last night. I got the answers I was looking for and I felt amazing knowing that it wasn't me that he'd been running from.

I reached for the door handle, but Miles stretched his hands over to grab my face. We looked at each other for a few moments and he dipped his head over mine to embrace my lips. It was a slow, toe-curling kiss that stole my breath straight out of my body.

"Talk later," he said as he kissed the tip of my nose.

I wanted to melt and tell Miles to screw it and turn back to his place. But I couldn't help thinking about the text that David had sent that was burning a hole in my purse.

Chapter Eighteen

I had a great time with Miles and Dillion at the beach. It also gave me the chance to get to know Kelly a little bit more, and her boyfriend, John. Kelly completely embarrassed Miles by telling me stories of when he was little and how Kelly used to dress him as a baby and play house. I couldn't get the image of Miles with footies and a pacifier in his mouth out of my head.

Miles was sweet and attentive, holding my hand when we walked along the lakeshore. Since the weather was warming up, it was still too cold to go swimming in the lake. Truth be told, I was glad, because I was convinced the lake was made up of sewer water from the whole Chicagoland area.

But, as promised, I did help Dillion make his Willis Tower of out sand, although in the end it looked more like a sand penis. I may have mentioned to Miles that I wanted to ride it, but he rolled his eyes and laughed.

Even though the day was incredible, I still had a twist in my stomach about David's text. I kept wondering what the hell he wanted to say that he hadn't spewed out before. I won't lie and say that my confidence hadn't taken a hit after our exchange. What was making it even worse was the text conversation I'd had with Martha earlier.

Martha the Miserable: Moxie, that email you sent me was deplorable. How could you possibly talk to your mother that way? I raised you better than that.

I wanted to be childish and go on a rampage about how she's not my mother, but I felt that it would be stooping to her level.

Moxie the Saint: Right, and the fact that you got a guy to GO OUT WITH ME so I'd lose weight puts you up for Step Mother of the Year.

Martha the Monster: That's not what I did. I simply told his mother that I have a single daughter who would be interested in getting to know someone in the health industry.

It was official. The woman was delusional. I wondered what it would take to have her deemed mentally unstable by the courts, so I could institutionalize her.

Moxie the Saint: Martha, if that's what you tell yourself to allow you to sleep at night, that's fine. Just remember this: when Yom Kippur comes around and you need to repent for your bad deeds, God will write you in the book of death.

Martha the Monster: You know I hate that prayer.
Moxie the Saint: And I hate guilt, so call it even.
Martha the Monster: Moxie, you're a beautiful girl, and losing
   some of those extra pounds will have the men trampling
   over themselves at your doorstep. Plus, we'll be able to go
   shopping at all the places you love.

I was not going to give in to this. I had Miles who loved me
the way I was inside and out. Right? Or was he just saying that
so I wouldn't feel bad? Sure, people loved my snarky attitude,
but was it enough to hold the interest of a man as beautiful as
Miles?

Moxie the Saint: Martha, I need to go. I have a plate of fried
   chicken waiting to be eaten, followed by a chocolate cake.

I flipped my phone off. Renee had said she was taking me
to someone's surprise party. I felt uncomfortable going to a
stranger's surprise party, but she swore to God that I would
enjoy it. Honestly, anything to get my mind off Martha and
David would help, and maybe they would have chocolate cake
there to soothe my soul.

Renee and I pulled up to a small house that had yellow
siding and a metal fence surrounding it. "This looks…homey,"
I said.

I decided not to tell Renee right away about sleeping with Miles. I was still trying to process everything in my own head.

"Sheila does my hair at Salon Envy and she invited me." Renee smiled as we walked through the metal gate.

"Whose birthday is it?"

"That's the fun part." She turned to look at me. "This isn't a birthday party."

"Please don't tell me we've been hired as strippers for a bachelor party. I haven't shaved my legs in a few days. I'm sure they wouldn't be happy with Cousin It from the Addams family."

"No. There are no men in there. Besides, do we need to have a discussion about female hygiene?"

Just as I was about to answer with a snarky comment, the door flew open. Standing there was a woman that I would have guessed was in her forties. She had blond, almost white, hair and a tan so fake that I needed sunglasses to look at her. Her bubble gum lipstick color matched her tiny mini dress. The look was completed with see-through six-inch-heel fuck-me shoes. I was now convinced that Renee had taken me to a class about becoming a prostitute.

"Renee!" she screeched.

"Hey, Sheila! Thanks again for the invite. This is my friend, Moxie." She moved her hand up and down me like she was giving a prize away on The Price is Right.

"Moxie! What a cool name. I'm so glad you're both here, and you are definitely in for a surprise," Sheila said while showing us inside the house.

Sheila's house looked like it had been picked up straight from Florida and plopped down in the middle of Chicago. The walls were painted peach and there was white leather furniture that a dozen women were crowded on. The artwork was paintings of the ocean and downtown Miami, but it was the neon flamingo that tied the whole theme together.

I whispered to Renee, "Is there some sort of Florida fetish thing going on here? We aren't here to hear a speech about renting a timeshare, are we, because Miami certainly wouldn't be my first choice."

"The house belongs to her mom, who is a snow bird. She's having the party here because she lives in a studio apartment in the city. I'll get us a glass of wine. Try getting us a good spot."

Utter confusion struck me as I tried to find a spot in-between two thirty-year-old women.

"Mind if we share this space?" I asked as I pointed to the space on the couch.

The brunette with dark eyes looked up at me. "Oh, Hun, scoot that ass of yours right here. Being in this spot gives us the best chance at prizes and also to see the merchandise up close."

"Who's the party for?" I questioned my new seat mate.

"It's for all of us, sweetie," she squealed and waved her hand around the room. "This is to benefit everyone. Haven't you ever been to one of these?"

I looked at her, disorientated. Of course I'd been to a surprise party in the past. But I wouldn't go as far as to say that it'd benefited me. In fact, I was always put out a few bucks after purchasing a gift. Renee came back and handed me a glass of white wine. However, it wasn't in a typical wine glass. It was a clear plastic cup that was long, with two balls that made up the base. Since my head lived in the gutter, my reaction was that it looked like a penis.

Sheila stood in front of the room and waved her hands, shushing everyone. "I would like to thank everyone for coming out tonight. You all have been so supportive of me making this transition, and I think it will be a huge hit."

Still confused, I whispered over to Renee, "Is she going through gender reassignment?"

She choked a little on her wine. "No."

Sheila continued to speak to the audience. "I hope you like everything I brought with me, and I know that a lot of you will be making some orders. We are going to play a little game to get started and to introduce ourselves."

She reached in a large black bag and pulled out what looked like a stuffed animal. She fidgeted with it for a moment until she figured out the proper way to present it.

It was a stuffed penis. It was pink and furry, like the stuffed animal poodle I used to sleep with at night. If the true goal of this party was to be surprised, I think Sheila just hit in on the head (no pun intended).

"We're going to pass around Pokey to each person. You have to share your name and favorite sexual position."

Sheila passed Pokey to the first girl on her left. "Hi, I'm Linda. I really prefer doggie style, but my husband said that he can't get off in the position, so he likes to have me ride him."

My mouth dropped. I am far from being an innocent person. In fact, sex is usually on my brain eighty percent of the day, the other being food and checking if I'd had a bowel movement that day. Yet, sitting in a room full of strangers, divulging information about my sex life seemed strange.

"What the fuck is this?" I whispered to Renee, who was engrossed in everyone's answers.

"It's a sex-toy party."

"Why the hell do they call it a Surprise Party?" I said, desperate for an explanation.

"It's kind of like a code name, so if you are discussing it in front of others they won't know what you're talking about."

As Renee was finishing her explanation to me, Mr. Pokey ended up in my lap. I picked up the fury stuffed penis, thinking it definitely needed to visit the salon for a wax. "Umm, hi, I'm Moxie." I paused, not really knowing how to continue. "I like to have sex and I don't discriminate between sexual positions. I feel they have their own unique qualities and deserve the right to be used at will."

The group looked at me like I was a contestant for the Miss America Pageant. But, in this case, it would be the Miss Missionary Position Pageant. I flipped Pokey over to Renee.

She jumped. "I recently started seeing someone who is Indian. He's big on the teachings of Kama Sutra and has been giving me homework assignments to learn them," she said with a smile before passing the penis to the next person.

"Is that true?" I leaned into her.

"Fuck, no. But I thought it was more exciting than telling them I make him put his head between my legs for hours. I didn't want to sound selfish."

Pokey Penis had made it around the entire group. I wondered if that penis had ever been fondled as much as tonight. Sheila grabbed the audience's attention again.

"Ok, gals, here's the fun part. We are going to bring out some toys!"

A petite woman on the other couch raised her hand as if we were in a classroom. "Will we get the chance to try the toys before making the decision to buy them?"

Who invited this woman? I think someone needs to be lead out of the party by the pussy police.

"No. There will be no testing of the products. However, you can turn the vibrators on and off to get an idea of their speed and pulse length."

I was about to make a comment when I felt something else vibrate. I was going to be impressed if she had a Blue Tooth vibrator that could send signals anywhere, but I was disappointed that it was just my phone.

I pressed my phone shut just as Sheila was talking about the different tasting lubricants.

"This one tastes like strawberries, which drives men wild."

Yes, I was sure the taste that mimics the smell of my Strawberry Shortcake doll was really a turn on. Well, unless you had a childhood toy fetish, for which you must seek therapy immediately.

One of the women in the group held up a clear ring in her hand. She inspected it closely, turning it around and squeezing it together.

"It's a cock ring," I said to her, hoping to give her some enlightenment.

The woman didn't even turn to me. She just replied, "I know it's a cock ring. Our baby chewed through our other one, so I was checking on the durability of this one."

That was when I heard that shrill voice that left my skin crawling. It was the high pitched squeal of Amber. What in fuck's sake was she doing here?

"Well, look who we have here. I didn't know the dog pound let its strays run around at night," she hissed.

I turned around to face her. "Slow night on the streets, or wouldn't any guys pick you up because of your bug-infested Cooch?"

"This is my cousin's house and I promised to stop by. And you know what's funny?" she asked with a smirk on her face. "Miles seemed to like my pussy when he had his tongue all over it. Oh, shit!" Her hands clasped over her mouth, pretending to have just revealed a secret. "He made me promise not to tell you."

My stomach jumped into my throat. "What?" I asked. I tried not to let my voice crack, but it did anyway.

"Yeah, he left your tent at the school camp-out and I saw him. I asked him if he was ok, but he just looked disgusted. He told me that you came onto him and forced him to make out with you. All he kept repeating was that he couldn't get over how your thighs kept jiggling and your tits sagged down to your knees. He said your cunt was so huge because of all the dicks you've slept with."

I was starting to feel the bile rise in my throat, but she continued talking.

"I felt so bad for him that I pulled him behind some bushes and asked him if he wanted to know what a real woman felt like. He was more than eager to find out. He gave me the best damn orgasm of my life. The man really knows how to work his tongue. He loved rubbing his hand up and down my thighs and kept saying I was everything a woman should be."

"You're fucking lying," I snarled.

"Really? How come he wasn't in your tent when you got up?"

"He took Dillion home because he was having a night terror."

"Did he actually say that to you or did you just assume that's why he left? He really left because he didn't want you to find out he was with me."

My mind instantly returned to that morning. Miles hadn't ever said that he left because of Dillion. All Renee told me was that they were gone by the time I woke up. I felt chills run up and down my body and I wanted to throw up. How could I have been so fucking stupid, to think that a man like Miles would want to be with me?

"It sucks being the sympathy fuck, doesn't it?" Amber looked at me with fake sympathetic eyes and rubbed a hand up and down my arm.

"Don't fucking touch me," I barked.

Before I knew it, Renee was by my side. "What's wrong?" She looked at Amber, then back to me, and saw the tears in my eyes.

"Nothing," I lied. "I think there is something wrong with the appetizers and it's affecting my stomach. We should probably get out of here." With that, we left the dildos and the trash behind.

Chapter Nineteen

I lay in bed looking at the ceiling, wondering when was the last time I cleaned, because I was spotting major cobwebs. I hadn't slept last night. Amber's words haunted me and I kept imagining her fake press-on Lee nails digging into Miles's skin in the throes of passion. Words floated in my mind, *thighs kept jiggling* and *tits sagged down to my knees.* I was going to vomit.

I couldn't believe Miles would jump from my tent that night into Amber's awaiting arms. Sure, I thought she was a rat-faced bitch, but I could see why men went after her. She was skinny, blond, and had big tits. The perfect Barbie doll. I was so stupid to think a man like Miles would ever be interested in someone like me. All those words he said to me the night we made love… But it wasn't making love, not by a long shot. It was let's-get-our-kicks-screwing-the-fat-chick.

I climbed out of bed and went into the kitchen to start my coffee. My purse sat on the counter and I heard it buzzing. I reached deep into the pocket and pulled out my phone. If things couldn't get worse…

"Morty's Mortuary, how may I help you?"

"Moxie, it's your mother."

I groaned, a little too deflated to go into the whole you're-not-my-mother discussion.

"Moxie Summers, I demand that you stop this foolish behavior," she said, in what tried to be an authoritative tone.

"Martha, I can't talk right now."

"Oh, now you don't even have time for your mother?"

I would gladly give my mother time if she were alive.

"You know, when I was younger I would never have treated my own mother this way."

"Martha, when you were younger you used to hang out at the temple and wait for widowers after they buried their wives."

"That is not true. I was simply there to provide refreshments to those who stayed after the services."

"Is that why Jane Singler caught you making out with Rabbi Schwartzman?"

"Young lady! That was many years before I met your father!"

"Martha, I've gotta go."

"And where do you think you're going?"

What was this? Was I twelve again? I hoped to hell not, because having my pubes grow in itched like a son of a bitch. I thought of something that would send her mouth foaming.

"I'm going to meet David at the coffee shop."

"What? This is great news! I'm so glad you saw it our way. He's going to make such a great impact on your life, Moxie."

There would definitely be impact.

"Sure, Martha. And then I'm going to shave my head and join a cult that likes to have sex with cows."

"Moxie!"

After I ended the call with Martha, I pulled up the texts inbox on the phone. I found David's last text asking me to meet with him. My head swam in confusion. I keyed in the letters and hit send.

Moxie: Fine. Meet me at the coffee house at six o'clock.

Ten minutes passed before I heard my phone beep.

David: You've finally come around. I'll be there, waiting.

I took a quick shower, hoping it would somehow revive me. While I let the water wash over me, I thought back on the last few days. I didn't know what David was going to say to me. Honestly, I didn't even know why I'd agreed to meet him. I was acting on impulse because I was so hurt about all the things that Amber had told me. It seemed that the only way Miles wanted me, was everything I was not.

After work, I rushed home to ditch the frazzled teacher look and get ready for my meeting with David. I walked into my closet thinking about what I wanted to wear. Certainly not anything sexy. Or did I? As with all major life decisions, I had to contact my fashion consultant. I pushed letters into my phone.

Moxie: Hey, Jizz Dribbler.

221

Ryan: Only when going down on multiple guys.
Moxie: That's really foul.
Ryan: You started it.
Moxie: What? Are you five?
Ryan: Excuse me, I had my sixth birthday yesterday.
Moxie: I need fashion advice.
Ryan: Why the hell do you always text asking for fashion advice?
Moxie: I slept with Miles.

I didn't want to tell Ryan what had transpired at the sex-toy party with Amber. I knew I would have gotten a lecture about how beautiful I was and where was my confidence. We would deal with that conversation later.

Ryan: Fine. Wear the black pants with the purple flowing top and yellow flats. Now spill.
Moxie: Meet me at Carlo's as soon as you can and we'll talk.
Ryan: Is he hung?
Moxie: Goodbye, Ryan.
Ryan: That means yes! SQUEAL!

I put the phone down and dug through my closet for my black jeans and purple top that Ryan had suggested. It was a good choice, as the jeans accented my curves and the top made my boobs look like ripe watermelons. It communicated the perfect message of *you fucking idiot, you could have had this luscious ass.*

I finished styling my hair and spritzed on some perfume, grabbed my keys and headed out the door. Mentally, I was preparing the speech I was going to give David. I was thinking about something along the lines of being a misogynistic prick and that I was going to send out a memo to all of womankind to not go out with him.

The coffee house was crowded with its usual after-workday crowd and I was lucky that my favorite barista was working. Maybe I could persuade her to put a whole bottle of stool softener in David's coffee.

"Hey, Moxie, what can I get started for you?" she said.

"Usual coffee with four cream and four sugars."

She hesitated for a minute and whispered, "Would you like some extra shots of espresso?"

"Are you my favorite barista?" I murmured as I reached over the counter to rub her baseball cap.

"Moxie?"

I turned around to see David standing there, dressed like he was going to a funeral. He had on a dark suit, white shirt and a blue tie. He was also holding a large bouquet of flowers.

"Who died?" I said in a deadpan voice.

"They're for you."

He reached out to hand me the flowers. I took them, turned back to the barista and gave her the bouquet.

"I told you that you were my favorite," I said sweetly to her, then I turned back to David.

"I deserve that," he said, looking down at his shoes.

"No, you deserve to be drawn and quartered, but my medieval minion is busy at the moment."

He laughed at that.

"Would you like to sit down?" he said, pointing to an empty table.

I took my coffee, which was ready, and headed to the table. I should have gotten a donut to eat in front of him, but I thought that would be petty. I would have to get the donut to go though.

"So what do you want, David? To let me know that you invented a new diet pill and you're looking for a poster child for the product?"

"I'm sorry," he said.

"You brought me all the way here to say that you were sorry?"

"That, and to say that I was wrong about you. You're kind, funny, and you're also beautiful."

Ok, that had me a little baffled. I thought the only reason he was trying to lure me in was to change my looks, and now he's calling me beautiful? This man needed serious psychiatric help.

"I have been living the past seven years with the notion that body image was everything. Working in the health industry, we have to maintain a certain image, because who is going to buy supplies from someone who's…"

"Who's what, David?" I narrowed my eyes at him.

"It's not coming out right. Let me start over. When we met the first night, yes, I went in there thinking that I could convince you to try the new diet system that we have. But, I started talking to you and I honestly enjoyed our conversation. I really like your honesty."

"What? Am I the first one to tell you to fuck yourself?"

"Actually, yes."

"Excuse me?"

"I grew up getting my way most of the time. Getting women was never something I struggled with. Women would come to chase me to go out. And then I met you and you had this feisty side that I found so sexy, I figured I would just get over your size."

I couldn't believe what I was hearing. This guy could not be for real. Why did I leave Miles and Dillion for this? What was I looking for? An apology? Great, I got it and now I could go.

"David, while this meeting has been enlightening, I'm going to stay with my original assessment and say go fuck yourself."

I stood up and took my coffee to head out the door when David blocked my way.

"I see I'm going to have to convince you another way," he said.

He reached for the sides of my face. He pulled me into him for a very sloppy, very detestable kiss. I put my hands up to his chest to push him away and then give him another kick in the balls, but before I could, I heard a very familiar voice.

"Moxie?"

I pushed off David to spin around and saw Miles standing there.

"Miles!" I cried. "It's not what it looks like."

David wrapped his arms around my waist, holding me close to him.

"Moxie, honey, why don't you tell this asshole that we're fucking each other?" David revealed a nasty smile at Miles.

"What? No…Miles…he's lying." I tried pushing out of David's hold, but he was too strong.

Miles stood there frozen, but it was as if he couldn't even hear what I was saying. He turned and pushed the door open to leave.

"Miles!" I screamed, trying again to get his attention. It didn't work, but I now had the attention of all the patrons of the café.

I became enraged. Everything that I wanted, that I dreamed of, just walked out the door, and I was encased in this asshole's arms. I had to go after Miles, to set this whole thing straight. First, I needed to take care of David.

I thought back to the defense class that Renee and I took. At the time, I thought it was ridiculous to punch and kick a sack full of flour, but now I was feeling grateful. I took my left foot, lifted it and stomped as hard as I could on David's foot. He yelled and loosened his grip around me enough for me to turn and send my elbow into his face. He shot back, holding his nose.

"You fat bitch!" he yelled.

"No, that's Miss Fat Bitch to you, ass wipe," I said , then took my leg and lodged it between his legs, making sure the chances of him ever procreating were slim.

The whole coffee house erupted in cheers and standing ovations. I was grateful for the support, but didn't have time to sign autographs. I needed to find Miles before it was too late.

Chapter Twenty

I can honestly say that I have never run so fast in my entire life. I did not understand the attraction of people who liked to run for pleasure, as my lungs felt like they were on fire. I saw the back of Miles's head and shouted out his name. He either didn't hear me or was ignoring me on purpose. I had a feeling it was the latter. I wasn't all that surprised at what a prick David was, I was more upset with myself for meeting him and getting into this mess.

I saw Miles get into his car and turn out into the street. I had to get to his sister's house and try to explain to him what happened. I turned back and headed to my apartment to get my car, not even excusing myself to the people I bumped into.

I got to my car in the parking garage and turned the key in the ignition. The noise my car made sounded like my grandma after smoking a pack of cigarettes.

"No! Not now, not now," I said to no one.

I hit the steering wheel with my hands and lowered my head. Out came the sound of the car horn, which in turn somehow set off the car alarm. I got out of the car and pressed the alarm button on the key fob. Suddenly, a large sound and puff came out the muffler. I used my foot and kicked the side of the car, calling it every profanity I could think of.

I hurried back to my apartment and called Renee.

"Hello," a male voice with a British accent answered.

"Raj?"

"Yes, ma'am."

"I didn't know that you and Renee were serious enough to be answering each other's phone. That's a four-month policy," I alerted him.

"Well, she's in the loo and I saw your caller ID, so I figured there must be some sort of crisis."

"I don't only call her in times of crisis, Raj."

"Right, but the chances of you and a crisis being intertwined are very likely."

He got me there.

"Tell Renee to get her ass out of the loo and get on the phone."

There were a few moments of silence and then Renee answered.

"Hello?"

"We have a DEFCON one happening and I need your car," I said so fast that I wondered if she even understood anything I'd just said.

"Moxie, relax. What happened?"

"Last night at the party Amber told me she and Miles slept together. She said that Miles was disgusted by my body and went to her for comfort."

"And now you're going to kill her, put her body in a car and push it over the bridge and into the water?"

"Listen, Snatchquash, we've got a real problem here."

"Ok, ok. What's up?"

"I slept with Miles," I revealed. "It was before Amber told me everything. So I was pissed and hurt, so I texted David to meet me at the coffee house."

"Oh, Moxie, you didn't," she groaned.

"I went because I wanted to tell him what a horrible human being he was. The scum of the earth, the toxic waste to clean water…"

"I get it! What happened next?"

"I argued with David and stood up to leave, and then he thought it would be a brilliant time to stick his tongue down my throat."

"Was it any good?"

"Renee, focus!"

"Sorry."

"Then Miles walked into the coffee house and saw us kissing. When I tried to explain to him what was going on, David wrapped his hands around me and told Miles we were screwing each other."

"Oh, shit. Definitely a DEFCON one."

"He ran out of the place before I got a chance to explain and I tried to follow him, but he moved too fast."

"We really need to get back on an exercise regimen."

"RENEE!" I hollered.

"So what happened to your car?"

"It met its ultimate demise."

"You should have gotten your maintenance on it done when I told you to."

She was lecturing me at a time like this?

"Seriously?" I said.

"Fine, come over and you can use my car."

"Thank you, I'll be over in five minutes."

I hung up the phone, got my keys and bolted out of my apartment. I was praying that Miles would hear me out and that David's dick would turn black, shrivel up and fall off. I felt awful for the woman who would have David as a boyfriend, but then again, there were a lot of mentally ill people out there who needed a companion as well.

Renee's apartment was only a few blocks from mine and when I got there I was completely out of breath from walking fast. I pressed the buzzer by the door for her apartment.

"Hello?" she answered.

"It's me."

"Damn, I was hoping it was the pizza delivery guy."

"Stop being a twat waffle and get your ass down here."

"Hostility is not becoming on you." She giggled.

After a few minutes, Renee came downstairs with her keys. She looked like she had been through the spin cycle of a washing machine.

"What the fuck happened to you?" I asked.

"Last night happened to me. Raj believes in Neotantra."

"Is that like whips and chains?"

"No, it's Tantric sex. And let's just say that I came in touch with my spiritual side," she said with a smug look.

I rolled my eyes and took the keys out of her hand.

"She's a block down on the left. And be gentle with her, I just had her detailed."

Renee was like a guy when it came to her car. It was an older Corvette that was redone and she treated it as if it was her first born. One time I dropped a French fry on the floor of the car after picking up McDonalds for lunch. I thought she was going to throw me out of the car on a moving highway.

"Love you!" I said, sprinting toward the car.

I found the house, pulled into the drive and opened the car door. I saw Miles's car there, so I knew he had come back. I ran up to the front door and knocked on it like I was a Jehovah's witness wanting to sell religion. Kelly opened the door.

"Hi, Moxie."

"Ok, it's not what it looks like."

She held up her hand to stop me.

"It is not my job to get tangled in my brother's business."

"Is he here?" I tried to peek inside.

"He is. I'll try to convince him to come out. He doesn't want Dillion hearing any of this."

"Ok, thanks."

I stood on the front stoop, twisting the bottom of my shirt in my hands. They felt clammy, like before I had to make a big speech in front of a group. The door opened and Miles stepped outside. He had disappointment in his eyes, which was so different from the light I saw in them the previous morning.

"Miles, I can explain…"

But like his sister, he put up his hand to stop me.

"Moxie, I told you two nights ago that I just don't sleep around with any girl that comes my way. I had feelings for you, but I can't put myself out there just to be set up. After what both Dillion and I have been through, it's just not fair."

Wait, excuse me? What the hell is he talking about? He's the one who ran into Amber's arms because he thought I was just some fraternity haze prank. Then he has the balls to go on and say he doesn't put himself out there and bring Dillion into it?

"What, are you going to tell me it was nothing?" he continued. "You were kissing him and he had his arms around you. He said that you were sleeping together. Why did you even find it necessary to meet him?" He crossed his arms against his chest in a defensive posture.

"He was lying!" I was practically screaming. "He said it to be spiteful because I wouldn't agree to be with him. I agreed to meet him to tell him what an asshole I thought he was. And like you're one to talk, shacking up with Amber at the camp-out because I apparently gross you out. Why did you even take it further, Miles, if you think I'm so hideous?"

"What?" he said softly. "I never hooked up with Amber."

"And you expect me just to believe you, like you so obviously believe me when I say nothing happened with David!"

"I have given you no reason whatsoever to make you believe I slept with Amber. I haven't even seen her since helping her with the fires at the camp-out. I also remember telling you that everything that you are what I want. But it takes one second of Amber screwing with you and you run straight to David instead of coming to me and talking it out. Why?"

"Because…I…" I trailed off, knowing that if I told Miles how insecure and horrible David and Amber made me feel he wouldn't understand.

I paused and looked at him. My heart sank. Everything I wanted was slipping out of my hands. I knew he was hurt and he felt I hurt Dillion, too. But I was hurt, too. I felt crushed that he didn't trust me enough to know that I wanted to be with him and no one else. Everything that had transpired in the last twenty four hours was starting to take a toll on my emotions.

I shrugged my shoulders and looked him in the eyes. All I could do at this point was protect myself and my heart. The words I said stung as they came out of my mouth.

"I guess I can't get over my slutty ways. You know, I can't be happy fucking just one guy. What's the fun in that?"

"Moxie…" he said softly and reached out for me, but I turned around and walked back to Renee's car.

I got into the car and backed away from the house. Miles was still standing on the front step, watching me, and even though it was breaking my heart, I had to get out of there. I turned the street corner and when the house was out of sight I put the car in park and let the tears flow down my face.

Chapter Twenty One

It had been three weeks since what I called D-day. Better known as Dickhead Day, because that was when Dickhead David ruined my life. Ok, maybe I had a hand in my love life's demise, too. I shouldn't have gone to meet with him. What I hadn't considered was how Miles felt, and I hadn't trusted in his feelings for me. Every day at school was a reminder of Miles thanks to his mini-me sitting in my class. Dillion and I never talked about what happened that day. I'm sure he felt burned and betrayed by me. I'd seen him at his most vulnerable point and now I bet he felt like I'd abandoned him.

I was sitting at my desk during lunch when Renee came into my class holding a donut bag and a Big Gulp.

"This is the last day that I'm tolerating this sinkhole that you've created," she said as she put the bag on my desk.

"It's not a sinkhole. It's a large, silent, dark abyss where soulless spirits float around in despair."

"It's a good thing that you're not dramatic," Renee said sarcastically.

"Seriously, I totally fucked things up with my own insecurities."

"Best thing to do is get back into the dating pool. What about online dating?"

I looked around the room to make sure that we were indeed alone and that Renee's evil twin hadn't walked in with her.

"Are you fucking insane? Online dating is for ugly, desperate people. They put a profile on there, and a picture that looks nothing like themselves. Then you go on the date and are met by the Hunchback of Notre Dame."

"So not true. I have a friend who met her husband through online dating."

"You have other friends?" I asked with a smirk.

"Yes and fuck you." She laughed.

"Who is this other friend?"

"Claire; you don't know her."

"I know all you friends," I said with suspicion.

"She's one of Raj's friends."

"Oh, so now his friends are your friends?"

"Moxie, you're trying to switch this on me and it's not working. Pull up Match Me.com."

I could not believe what I was about to do. My heart was still broken over Miles and I was going to try online dating? A colonoscopy would have been more exciting. Even though Miles and I were never officially a couple, I couldn't help feeling like this was cheating on him in some way. But Renee was determined that I get back on the horse, and knowing Renee, she wasn't going to back down until I did it.

She pulled a chair next to me at my desk as I switched the computer on. I typed in the website address and groaned.

"This is such a bad idea."

"Look at it this way: you can stalk men's pictures and flirt with them online. No one is making you marry the first guy you talk to."

The home page of Match Me was filled with a loving couple kissing and walking hand in hand on the beach. Seriously? If I wasn't afraid I'd lose the Snickers bar I'd just consumed, I might have vomited all over the computer.

"You need to set up a profile," Renee said as she tore the computer away from me.

She went into member profile set up and started working away while I was plotting my escape from the country. She paused and looked at me.

"What's your favorite type of food?"

"That's like asking someone what their favorite appendage is, their arm or their leg."

"I'll put tacos."

"Don't put tacos!" I yelled.

"Why not?"

"Because they'll think that I like girls."

"What?" Renee asked, looking at me like I lost my mind.

"You know, that's another way to say pussy. Pink Taco."

"Have you ever considered seeking professional help?" she said laughing.

"That ship sailed long ago, trust me," I sighed.

"Fine, I'll put brownies." She went to start typing it in. I grabbed the keyboard.

"Don't put that in either, they'll see my picture and think that I sit around all day stuffing brownies in my mouth. Let me do it," I said, looking over the questions.

I wasn't serious about this at all. I was merely doing it to get Renee off my back. I told her that I would finish the profile and go searching for available stud muffins as soon as it was complete. With a smile and a look of satisfaction, she got up from the chair and headed back to her class. Since I had a planning period after lunch, I had more time to look at this site before my kids came back to taunt me.

I looked over the questionnaire in front of me and decided that if Renee was going to make me do this, then I was going to have a little fun with it.

Name?

MoxieAnn Burtha Summers

What's your Sign?

I like to think of myself as a stop sign, but people might think of me as more of a yield.

What's your Favorite Food?

Ram's penis in its own sauce.

What's your favorite TV show?

Murder She Wrote, because it gives me ideas.

What is your idea of a perfect first date?

First, my date will take me to McDonalds, but it has to be one with a playground. My date orders a happy meal for me, but upgrades the drink to a shake because I don't want him to go cheap. We sit on the Mayor McCheese slide in the play area and kick out little snotty kids who are looking to have a good time. After that, I expect my date to take me home to scrub my feet and remove the calluses with a cheese grater. After I pop my pimples while he watches, I expect him to put out or get out.

What qualities are you looking for in someone?

That he has a heartbeat and fresh smelling breath.

What are your best qualities?

If I had good qualities, then why the hell would I be on here when I probably could get laid elsewhere?

What was your most embarrassing moment?

According to my mother, after I was born I took a shit all over the doctor. Followed closely to the time I got caught feeling up the girls in the fifth grade, trying to see what those weird bumps were, growing from our chests.

What does your typical Saturday morning look like?

I have no idea. I'm usually too hung over from partying on Friday night and sleep until 2:30 on Saturday afternoons.

Do you have a religious preference?

I prefer someone who worships sheep.

What do you do for fun?

I like to roll around with pigs in their own shit. If I'm feeling particularly spontaneous, I might take a crap in there as well.

Do you follow politics?

Yes. Oh, wait, I misread it. I thought it said does the police follow you.

If you won the lottery, how would you spend your millions?

Buying a room full of good looking men to screw so I wouldn't have to do this online crap.

Any final comments?

Life sucks.

I found a picture of myself in my files that Ryan took when we were at Navy Pier last summer. We were in the beer garden and I had a few beers in my system. I was making this really unappealing face with my fingers stuck in my nose. It was perfect. It pretty much said everything I was feeling about doing this online bullshit. I figured this was a sure fire way to make sure no one contacted me and I could still tell Renee that at least I'd tried. I hit the finished button in the profile and away it went.

I still had a little bit of time left so I figured I would rummage through other people's profiles. I didn't have any interest in contacting anyone, but it was interesting to see how desperate other people could be.

For example, we have Chet. Chet likes long walks along Lake Michigan, riding in a carriage down the Magnificent Mile and spoiling his date by taking her to dinner at Trump Tower.

And then there's Steve. Steve likes to get down and dirty with a girl who likes sports and is a major White Sox Fan. There is even a picture of him humping the Commissioner's Trophy when they won the World Series.

I was about to shut my laptop when I heard a little ding sound and an instant message popped up. A man named Michael was contacting me.

Michael: Hi

I looked around the room as if he were talking to someone besides me. There was no way I could possibly attract someone with the profile I created. I stared at the screen for a few seconds before responding.

Moxie: Hi
Michael: How are you?
Moxie: Fine, thanks. And you?
Michael: You have an interesting profile.
Moxie: Well, if you're looking for psychotic, you found it.
Michael: You're very funny and cute.
Moxie: Are we talking about the same profile picture?
Michael: If it's the one with your fingers up your nose, then yes.

I realized at that moment I had no idea what this guy looked like. I moved the mouse over his name in the chat box and his profile appeared. He wasn't bad looking, but I wouldn't say that he was out of this world gorgeous either. It said he was 5'8". He had blond hair and glasses, a big nose, but a nice smile that seemed sweet. The picture was of him sitting behind a desk, maybe at his work. He wore a white polo shirt and from his profile he was thirty eight years old. The fact that he liked my profile pretty much indicated that he was mentally unstable.

Michael: You still there?
Moxie: Yes, I was checking out your profile. Only fair, since
  you've seen mine.
Michael: True.

> Moxie: So out of all the other people on this site, what made you choose mine?
> Michael: You're original. I like that. Plus, I kind of figured everything that you wrote probably isn't true. Except maybe the part about eating at the McDonald's playground.
> Moxie: You got me. But the truth is I totally have a thing for Grimace.
> Michael: I have a confession.
> Moxie: What is that?
> Michael: I had a huge crush on Birdie Early Bird when I was a kid.

I laughed out loud, but immediately felt guilty. I shouldn't find other guys attractive or laugh at their lame jokes. I wanted to laugh at Miles's stupid jokes and lay in his big arms. But Miles was the one thing I couldn't have and at least Michael was providing some entertainment for the time being.

> Michael: So, what are some real qualities that you are looking for in someone?

I paused. He was turning the conversation serious and I didn't know if I wanted serious. I could lie. Chances were I would never meet this guy. It might be therapeutic to talk to a complete stranger. There is something about being behind a computer that makes it easier to say things. It certainly would be a lot cheaper than therapy. My computer chimed.

> Michael: Did I already scare you off? If it helps, I can go first.

Moxie: Sure, enlighten me.

Michael: Ok. I'm looking for a woman who is sweet, but also sassy. That's why your profile caught my eye. Someone who doesn't take themselves too seriously, but knows when to get down to business and doesn't take shit from anyone.

Moxie: How do you know I'm that kind of girl? I could be a boy pretending to be a woman, but maybe I'm a zebra really trying to be a man, trying to be a woman.

Michael: You lost me.

Moxie: I was just making sure everyone was still awake after your moving speech on what makes the perfect woman.

Michael: Hmm, seems as though we have a woman scorned on our hands.

Damn. I was being a total bitch with this poor guy when all he was trying to do was be nice.

Moxie: Sorry, I just got out of a bad…relationship.

Michael: Ah, the broken heart.

Moxie: Something like that.

Michael: Want to talk about it?

I thought about it. Did I really want to pour out my sob story to this stranger? My kids started to trickle in the classroom, answering the question for me.

Moxie: I have to get back to work.

Michael: Maybe we can chat again?

Moxie: Yeah, maybe.

Leaving the conversation there, I snapped my laptop shut. I saw Dillion walk into the room and I couldn't help but feel like I was cheating on Miles by talking to Michael. I looked at Dillion and gave him a smile, but all I got back was sad eyes. It was like he saw right through me.

Chapter Twenty Two

When I got home from teaching I was wiped. There must have been a full moon, because my kids had been complete terrors today. Well, they were terrors every day, but someone must have given them all Jolt before class today. Katie took it upon herself to alert the class that the girl scouts were going on a field trip to the Zoo and I wasn't invited because I was prejudiced towards the panda bear race. That was when I slipped a dead bug into her snack.

There was a knock on the door and my heart immediately sped up. Was it possible that Miles would come by after all this time? Ok, it had been three weeks, but it felt like months had gone by. I went to answer the door, and if it was someone trying to sell me a religion, I was going to tell them that Jesus was already here and possessed me with the power to send them to hell.

"You look pathetic!" Ryan said as I opened the door. "And don't you ask who's at the door before answering? I could have been a murderer."

"I would accept a murderer, unless you were one that sold the word of God."

"You've really lost it, you know that, don't you?" he said as he glided into my apartment.

"Please, come in," I said with sarcasm.

"Bitch, please. I have a free pass to come into this place whether you like it or not."

"How may I be of service to you, Lord Ryan?"

He turned around to eye me, then he stood and opened his arms wide as an invitation. I sauntered over to him and buried my head in his neck, taking a deep breath of his smell. He wrapped his large arms around me and kissed the top of my head.

"You ok?" he whispered.

"If I told you I wasn't, would you have a magical cure?"

"The only thing that I could possibly get you that is magical is some 'shrooms."

"I'm allergic to fungus."

"You went out with that guy Chris and he had fungus growing on his tongue, remember?"

"He had a case of thrush on his tongue."

"Yeah, wasn't it from licking his own balls?"

I let out a belly laugh. It felt good. Ryan had a special way of making me feel better. The feeling didn't rival that of being with Miles, but I would accept it nevertheless. I decided to ask some questions I knew I didn't want answers to, but I couldn't help it.

"How is he?"

Ryan and I moved to the couch and sat down. I could tell that he was a little uncomfortable with me asking. But since Ryan saw him at work, he was instantly put in the middle.

"He's fine."

"Fine?"

"Yeah."

"What does that mean, fine?"

"It means he's fine."

"Ryan, is he moping around the office? Is he out partying with friends? Is he bringing girls home and fucking them, pretending they're me?"

"First of all, I wouldn't have a fucking clue whom he's bringing home because, against popular belief, I don't stalk him. Second, I don't follow him at the office because I do this thing called work and he sits in a different part of the department."

"Well, what kind of friend are you? You're supposed to be spying on him for me."

"Moxie, I know you're hurt and upset, but other people have lives going on and we can't stitch back together what you broke."

I stood there stunned.

"What did you say?" I asked him, hoping I'd misheard him the first time. "Are you saying this is all my fault?"

"No, there is equal fault here. But you let your insecurities get the better of you. There was no reason that you should have gone to see David. You had a good thing going and you fell back into old habits. You let your stepmother win this war."

"What does my stepmom have to do with this?" I barked.

"She has everything to do with this, Moxie. You claim to love how you look and that you are comfortable with who you are. But when Martha plants one seed of doubt in your mind, you destroy any self confidence you have."

"She isn't the one who said those awful things to me Ryan, David did." I was really becoming angry with this situation.

"David might have said the words, but it was really Martha who could have been saying them. She has never been happy with who you are. David was just a way to get at you."

Tears started to leak from my eyes. Ryan was right, it was really Martha who hurt me and David was the way in which see did it. Sure, I needed to take responsibility for my own actions, which meant the part about not trusting Miles. I knew there had to be a lot to do with my relationship with my stepmother, but those were not emotions that I could deal with at that moment.

"I'm sorry," I said as I slumped into Ryan's open arms.

He kissed the top of my head. "It's ok. I want you to be happy and you need to know that you are beautiful inside and out. Really start believing in yourself, Moxie, and relationships will bloom into something beautiful and honest."

"Thanks, Dr. Phil," I said, mocking him.

He changed his voice to a deep southern drawl, like Dr. Phil's. "Know you, young lady, better snap out of it or I'll put you over my knee and spank you."

"I didn't know that Dr. Phil was into BDSM," I said in a full-blown laugh.

Ryan ended up staying while we ordered pizza and watched the Keeping up With the Kardashians on TV. It was a dirty secret that Ryan and I watched the show. I always talked about how much I hated them, but I could never miss out on a single episode. After we cleaned up dinner and Ryan left, I went to my laptop and turned it on. I checked my email and Facebook like always, and then went to the Meet Me website. I didn't know what I was doing there; I didn't have any interest in meeting anyone. But there was a small part of me that was curious about this Michael guy. A bolt of guilt hit me instantly, thinking about Miles.

I saw that Michael was online and I hovered over the chat box, wondering if I should send him a message. Before I knew what I was doing, I hit send.

Moxie: Hi.

A few minutes passed and I scolded myself for being such an idiot and messaging him. I was about to close my laptop when I heard a chime.

Michael: Hey there.
Moxie: Sorry, I didn't mean to disturb you if you were in the process of doing something. You're probably chatting with multiple girls at once.
Michael: No, I was just cleaning up after dinner. I've only contacted you, so no other chats going on.

Oh, I wasn't expecting that comment. Why did he only contact me? My profile was the least inviting. Maybe this guy was into Goth chicks who lived in dark rooms and ate rats for snacks. Michael responded before I could type anything.

Michael: So what are you doing?
Moxie: Getting ready for beer pong.
Michael: Really? Did you know that I am the national beer pong champ?
Moxie: I'm pretty sure every frat boy in the country tries to claim that title.
Michael: Yeah, but they say it to try to get into girls' pants.
Moxie: And you?
Michael: Saying it to get into girls' pants ;)
Moxie: So Michael, what is it that you do for a living?
Michael: I work with my hands.
Moxie: Ok, now THAT sounds like a line a guy would use to get into a girl's pants.
Michael: Hmm. How about I like to create things?
Moxie: Interesting. Cryptic, but interesting.
Michael: And you?
Moxie: I teach elementary school.
Michael: I bet you make a great teacher.

I paused to look at that last sentence. This guy didn't know a thing about me. It was pretty presumptuous for him to think I would be a good teacher.

Michael: So you like kids?

I thought of Dillion and how his sweet smile would greet me in the mornings.

Moxie: Yeah, I guess I do.
Michael: So earlier you were telling me about a guy that broke
  your heart.

Suddenly, we went from fun banter to serious discussion. I didn't know how much I wanted to share with this stranger.

Moxie: What makes you think he broke my heart? I could have
  been the one to stomp all over his internal organs.

I felt myself getting defensive.

Michael: I have no doubt in my mind that you did. Something
  tells me you might have ripped out his heart and served it
  back to him on a silver platter.
Moxie: He kind of deserved it.
Michael: How so?
Moxie: He didn't trust me.
Michael: He didn't trust you or you didn't trust yourself?

Whoa. I looked around the room to see if there was a secret camera hiding somewhere. This guy was hitting things a little too close to home. But for some weird reason, I continued.

Moxie: It was a bit of both. He didn't trust in the fact that I was falling in love with him and I didn't want to be with anyone else. And I didn't trust myself to let him reciprocate the feelings. I had self-esteem issues and I thought he wouldn't understand.

Michael: Did you even give him a chance to try to understand?

Moxie: No, I didn't. He was a good guy. I should have given him the chance. I think he would have.

Michael: Well, this guy sounds like a complete asshole for letting you go without a fight.

I couldn't help but smile.

Michael: I know this sounds forward, but I would really like to meet you for coffee. No expectations, I can tell you're still healing. You seem like a nice person to know. And it doesn't hurt that you're beautiful.

My first reaction was to say no and snap the computer closed, but there was just something about this guy that drew me in. Maybe it was because I was feeling lost without Miles and I was looking for something to fill the void. I couldn't see a reason why I couldn't meet him one afternoon for coffee.

Moxie: Sure, we can meet for coffee.

Michael: How's this Sunday at one?

Moxie: That works. Anywhere special?

Michael: There is a coffee shop across from the Art Institute on Michigan Avenue and Adams.

My stomach dropped a little. The Art Institute was one of the places I was supposed to go with Miles and Dillion. I didn't want that reminder, but I also didn't want to be a wet blanket when this guy was going out of his way to be nice to me.

Moxie: Ok, well, I'll see you then, I guess.
Michael: I'm looking forward to it.

I shut off my computer and got ready to go to bed. But I lay in my bed staring at the ceiling, feeling that I was somehow betraying someone who was not even mine to betray.

Chapter Twenty Three

I woke up Sunday morning feeling slightly anxious. I still wasn't sure about meeting Michael for coffee. I needed some words of wisdom, so I called the person who put me in this predicament in the first place.

"Hello?" Renee answered in a sleepy tone.

"I need help."

"I'm glad that you have finally come to that conclusion. Do you want me to see if I can call the rehab place where all the stars go?" She laughed.

"Listen, sloppy tits, it's your fault that I'm having a panic attack."

"What happened?"

"I'm going on a date. Well, not a date, a get-together. With a stranger," I said, speaking so fast my words were combining.

"Wait, slow down. You're going on a date?"

"Sort of. This guy Michael I met on Meet Me asked me to get a coffee with him."

"Wow. That's amazing. I thought you told me you wrote a bunch of shit for the profile."

"What? I didn't tell you that. How do you know I did that?"

"Umm." There was a short pause on the phone. "I just know you so well, and I know that is something you would do."

"Well, I put something on there so you would get off my back. I certainly wasn't planning on meeting with anyone. But this guy messaged me anyway and we talked a little bit. I told him I wasn't looking for anything and that I just got out of a…thing."

"A thing?"

"Well, Miles and I were never officially a couple, so it was a Thing."

"So what's this THING you're going on today?"

"It's not a THING, it's coffee," I said sternly.

"Just go and have coffee, then. What's the worst that can happen?"

"That he will be a lunatic murderer who takes out my organs to sell on the black market!"

"In the middle of the coffee shop? Doubtful," she said.

"I'll have you know that my organs are worth a shit load of money. Ok, the ones that don't have a fat layer surrounding them."

We both broke out laughing. "Seriously, Renee, what am I doing?"

"Moxie, it's coffee. You're not signing your soul to the devil. Go out and have fun. Plus, you're putting Dunkin

Donuts out of business without getting your daily 'medication'."

"Fine, but if a body goes missing on the news tonight, I hope your guilt will live with you until your final moments."

"Moxie, I'm friends with you. You've already told me that I'm going to die of Jewish guilt by association."

"True. Promise me that we'll be buried together."

"Promise. Go, have fun and call me after. If I don't hear from you I'll send out the hounds."

I hung up the phone and went to get ready for my "Thing".

I stood in front of the coffee place on Michigan and Adams. Panic seeped in and I wanted to run the other way. I was still trying to find validity for being here. I should be home, in my pajamas, getting a tub of ice cream, sulking at how pathetic my love life is. Actually, I just wanted to lay down and think about how much I missed Miles. But this was my first step in moving on. I blew it with Miles and now it was too late. I decided to put my big girl panties on and head into the coffee shop.

"Welcome to Starbucks. What can I get started for you today?"

I looked at the friendly barista, wondering if I could con her into putting extra espresso into my drink. Maybe if I tell her I'm on a blind date she'll feel bad for me and give me some sisterly love.

"I'll take a large coffee, please."

"Do you mean a grande or a venti?"

I eyed her in confusion. I spoke slower, thinking that English might not be her first language.

"I…would…like…a…large…cofffffeeee."

She points to the cups. "Ma'am, we either have grande or venti."

"Fine, I'll take the venti with extra cream and sugar."

"Ma'am, you can add your own cream and sugar over there, at the bar."

"What kind of establishment is this?" I said a little too loudly.

"Ma'am, this is Starbucks."

"I fucking know it's Starbucks!" I gave her my credit card to pay for my coffee, which I would have been better off making at home.

I looked around to see if there was anyone that matched Michael's picture. There were quite a few people there, but no one that matched the picture on his profile. I found a seat and took out my phone. I wanted to look like I was busy texting or reading something, so I didn't look like I was desperately waiting for him to show.

"Order up for Moodle," called the barista. For a moment I thought she purposely screwed up my name because I was a little short with her. I groaned and went to collect my coffee. She was so not getting a tip from me.

"Moxie?"

I spun around and almost dropped my coffee at what I saw. Miles.

"Miles, what are you doing here?" Everything inside me started to panic. What would happen if Michael showed up while Miles was here? My stomach started to feel unsettled.

"Do you need help?" He could see that my hands were shaking around my coffee.

"No, I…um…sugar." I pointed to the bar housing the cream and sugar. I walked briskly over there, trying to ignore the fact that he was following me.

"It's good to see you," he said softly. I looked around to see if Michael came in.

"Umm, yeah, you too," I said, pouring cups of cream and sugar into my coffee.

"Are you meeting someone?"

Oh, crap. "Yes," I mumbled.

"Can we sit and talk?" he asked.

Was he crazy? He wanted to sit down and have a fireside chat with me while I waited for my date or whatever the hell it was?

"Miles, now is not a good time."

"Just a few minutes. Then I'll be out of your hair."

I should be so lucky. I pointed to the chairs in the back and we walked back to have a seat. I kept my eye out for Michael.

"So how have you been?" Miles asked.

"Fine, thanks."

He let out a small laugh.

"Fine? That's it?"

"Yup, just fine." I was clutching my coffee like it was going to run away from me.

"So who are you meeting?"

Well, there was the Miles I got to know. Big set of balls.

"Not your concern," I sneered.

"I can tell you why I'm here," he continued.

"Don't really care," I lied.

"I was going over to the Art Institute to look at some art."

"Good for you."

"You know why I love art?"

"No, and I don't care." I was still lying.

"Because I love to create things with my hands."

I swear I stopped breathing. I looked Miles straight in the eyes. "What did you say?"

"I love to create things with my hands. And do you know who one of my favorite artists is?"

"No," I whispered.

"Michael Angelo."

Like a lightning bolt, the pieces fell into place. His favorite artist was Michael Angelo…the name Michael.

"Michael?"

Miles just sat in his chair, looking at me, smiling like he just let out the world's biggest secret.

"You're Michael? But how? There was no way for you to know that I was on that site."

"I knew you didn't want to talk to me. So Ryan had the idea to set up a fake profile on Meet Me. Then we got Renee involved and she said she would take care of getting you on there. Renee called me when you set up your profile and I searched for it. As they say, the rest is history."

"But what about the picture? Who was that?"

"That's Kyle. He works in Ryan's department at the network. He said we could use his picture for the profile."

I sat and gawked at Miles. I wasn't sure how to feel about all this. He went to great lengths to get into contact with me, but at the same time I was angry that he lied and I poured my heart out to him.

"Can we get out of here? Maybe go walk around the museum and talk?"

"Umm, sure." I got up, but my legs were shaking.

Miles took my hand and we walked out into the city's spring air. We walked across the street and entered the museum. After Miles paid our admissions, we started walking around the exhibits. At first we walked silently, looking at the art. Finally Miles broke the silence.

"I handled everything poorly. I should have listened to everything you wanted to say."

I tried to interject. "No, wait, listen. I got upset because I thought that you didn't want to be with me after you ran off to talk to David. That somehow you were rejecting me and Dillion. I was so scared because I thought no one would want a widower and a child who suffers from PTSD. I went into protection mode for Dillion's sake, but I didn't even give you the chance to explain. We both have insecurities and I was so locked down with mine that I never thought that you would have your own issues to battle."

Tears started to cloud my eyes. He turned to face me and grabbed both of my hands.

"I was wrong," he said. "But you should have talked to me and told me what was going on. I might not have initially understood, because all I see is a beautiful, strong, amazing woman. But I would have listened, and we could have talked about it."

Now the tears were streaming down my face. Miles pulled me close and kissed my cheeks where the tears were falling.

"Moxie, I want you to be a part of me, part of Dillion. We've waited for you to come into our lives. I made the mistake of letting you go once, but now there are no more mistakes because I am falling in love with you." He took my face in his hands and his blue eyes looked deep into mine. "I want you to be with us."

My heart exploded. I wrapped myself around him and pulled him as tight as I could around me. I pulled back just enough so our faces came close together. I slowly pressed my lips to his and felt the warm heat flow through us.

"I'm falling in love with you too, and there is nothing I want more than to be with you."

I fell back into his arms for another long hug, but broke it when something dawned upon me.

"What about Dillion? Shouldn't he have a say in this? He must hate me for walking out on him," I said with pain in my voice.

"You can ask him yourself." Miles smiled and looked over my shoulder.

I turned to see Dillion run up to us. "Miss Summers!" he yelled. Kelly was standing back, waving to us. Miles waved and mouthed "Thank you" to his sister, who turned around and left.

I crouched down to meet Dillion in the eyes. "Dillion, I am so sorry about walking out on you like that. Please know that every day I saw you in class my heart was breaking."

"I know, Miss Summers. Daddy said I couldn't talk to you about it at school because he was plotting a way to bring our damsel back to our castle," he said in his squeaky voice.

I looked up at Miles and eyed him for putting me through the torture of not being able to talk to Dillion. All he could do was giggle and shrug. I turned my attention back to Dillion.

"I want you to know that I love your daddy and I love you too, buddy. I would be honored if you would let this princess back into your castle."

"Miss Summers, you never left my castle."

I threw my arms around Dillion and squeezed him tight. The love of these two men was enough to pull any of my insecurities out and leave them behind. I stood up and Miles took one hand while Dillion took my other.

"Come on, boys. There are paintings with pinched nipples with our names on them," I said and walked hand in hand with the loves of my life.

Epilogue

It is September now and the temperature in Chicago is changing. Fall has always been my favorite season, even if it means going back to school. This year I've been bumped up to teach first grade, which means another year of having to deal with girl scout psycho Katie.

Miles and I have been together for five months and they have been the best months of my life. Miles finally bought a house out in the suburbs of Chicago. He said that he didn't want Dillion growing up with buildings instead of green grass around him. I wasn't such a fan of this, considering Chicago traffic took forever, but it gave me a good chance to have phone sex with him while I waited for the cars to move.

It was a Saturday afternoon and we were having an end of summer barbecue with friends at the new house. Renee, of course, brought Raj, as the two of them were going strong. Renee even mentioned to me that they were discussing moving in together. Secretly I was jealous, because I would have loved to live with Miles and Dillion.

Ryan came into the house, followed by Tom and their new pit bull, Chanel. Poor dog didn't stand a chance of having a heterosexual life with a name like that. Tom even bought him a pink collar with rhinestones on it. Dillion loved that dog and he would sit next to him and explain the history of the Roman Empire, while Chanel just sat there, drooling all over Dillion's pants.

After the whole fiasco with Martha, I cut our communications to a minimum. When I needed to talk to my dad, I called him directly on his cell phone, hoping that I could cut out talking to Martha altogether. I hadn't taken Miles to meet them yet. I was afraid Martha would scare him off and tell him that it was HIS people who killed Jesus and to stop blaming the Jews for everything.

I was in the kitchen, getting the hot dogs ready, when I heard Miles sneak up behind me.

"I would love to put my hot dog in your bun," he whispered in my ear.

"What would you say if I put on a strap-on hot dog and put it in your buns?" I teased, turning around to face him.

He engulfed me into his arms and planted a panty dripping wet kiss on my mouth.

"While I like our toys in the bedroom, there will be no strap-on of any sorts added to the mix," he confirmed.

"Damn, I hope the company I got it from takes returns."

Miles pulled back from our embrace and eyed me nervously.

"Relax, I'm kidding!"

He let out the breath he was holding in.

"Anyways, I got the ball gag for you to wear instead," I smiled.

Miles swatted my ass. "Behave, you wicked wench." We both laughed.

Dillion came bouncing into the kitchen. "Are we going to eat soon? I'm famished!"

"Yup," I said. "Your dad was just pulling the hot dogs off the grill. Did you eat all those cheese balls I put out on the table?"

"Yeah, but then Uncle Ryan told me that I needed to stay away from the balls that were hairy. What does he mean?"

Miles and I looked at each other, but instead of outrage all we could do was laugh and smile.

Acknowledgments

I can honestly say that I never thought I would get to a point where I would write an acknowledgments page. Why? Because I never thought this book would actually happen. It started out as a way to get what in Yiddish is called "shpilkes" or nervous energy out. I started writing short clips and posting them on a blog. A lot of people enjoyed reading them and I got the crazy notion that there were people that shared my sense of humor and would enjoy what Moxie had to offer.

First, to my mentor, friend, sounding board and all around great gal, Nadine Silber. You have given me all the tools that I needed to make this book become a reality. You were patient and walked me through every single step, showing me what it means to be a true author. When I first contacted you about romantic comedy writing, you never hesitated helping me and never treated me like I was some little person on the totem pole. Thank you for all your help.

Thank you to Ella Medler, who patiently read through every line of Moxie with a fine tooth comb making sure that I dotted all my i's and crossed all the t's. It's takes a mighty woman to edited my writing and my husband thanks you, since he was forced to edit all my graduate papers for me.

To the group who urged me on to write, the S'muffins. All of you encouraged me to take my craziness and turn it into writing. You're a sisterhood of smutty women that deserve to achieve every dream. Including getting David Gandy naked in your bed. To my Three Chicks with Dicks, what can I possibly say but that I love you. You've provided me with wonderful support, whether it was listening to me bitch or laughing about everyday things. To the two people who made up the character of Renee, she wouldn't have come to fruition if the two of you weren't in my life.

Thank you to my family for always allowing me to chase crazy dreams, and there have been many. Thank you to my husband Craig for supporting this endeavor and funding the enormous Kindle bill that sparked my interest in writing. You always said I could do anything, except the laundry, dishwasher, cleaning the counters, folding…

And finally, to my beautiful son. May you never read this book. But if you do, there is a large sum of money stashed away for your therapy bills.

Thank you for reading The Chronicles of Moxie. You can follow Z. B. Heller at

Email: zbhellerbooks@gmail.com
Website: www.zbhellerbooks.com
Facebook: https://www.facebook.com/pages/ZB-Heller
Twitter: @zbheller
Goodreads:
https://www.goodreads.com/author/show/7948170.Z_B_Hell
er

14811559R10156

Made in the USA
San Bernardino, CA
05 September 2014